Catherine Spencer

THE FRENCH COUNT'S PREGNANT BRIDE

EXPECTING!

She's sexy, successful and PREGNANT!

D0039806

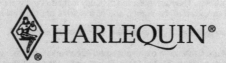

HARLEQUIN®

TORONTO • NEW YORK • LONDON
AMSTERDAM • PARIS • SYDNEY • HAMBURG
STOCKHOLM • ATHENS • TOKYO • MILAN • MADRID
PRAGUE • WARSAW • BUDAPEST • AUCKLAND

ISBN-13: 978-0-373-12578-4
ISBN-10:   0-373-12578-X

THE FRENCH COUNT'S PREGNANT BRIDE

First North American Publication 2006.

Copyright © 2006 by Spencer Books Limited.

www.eHarlequin.com

Printed in U.S.A.

All about the author...
Catherine Spencer

Some people know practically from birth that they're going to be writers. **CATHERINE SPENCER** wasn't one of them. Her first idea was to be a nun, which was clearly never going to work! A series of other choices followed. She considered becoming a veterinarian (but she lacked the emotional stamina to deal with sick and injured animals), a hairdresser (until she overheated a curling iron and singed the hair off the top of her best friend's head, the day before her first date), or a nurse (but that meant emptying bedpans!). As a last resort, she became a high school English teacher, and loved it.

Eventually, she married, had four children and, always, always a dog or two or three. How can a house become a home without a dog? In time, the children grew up and moved out on their own and she returned to teaching, but a middle-aged restlessness overtook her and she looked for a change of career.

What's an English teacher's area of expertise? Well, novels, among other things, and moody, brooding, unforgettable heroes: Heathcliff, Edward Fairfax Rochester, Romeo and Rhett Butler. Then there's that picky business of knowing how to punctuate and spell, and all those rules of grammar. They all pointed her in the same direction: breaking the rules every chance she got, and creating her own moody, brooding unforgettable heroes. And that's where she happily resides now, in Harlequin Presents novels, of course.

PROLOGUE

8:00 p.m., November 4

FOR once, Harvey arrived at the restaurant ahead of her, already settled in their favorite corner. She left her satin-lined cashmere cape with the hat-check girl, smiled at the sweet-faced, very pregnant young woman perched on a bench near the front desk and threaded her way through the maze of other diners to where he sat. Twenty-eight red roses, one for each year of her life, and a small package professionally gift-wrapped in silver foil and ribbons, occupied one end of the linen-draped table; a bottle of Taitinger Brut Reserve chilling in a silver champagne bucket and two crystal flutes, the other.

"Am I late?" she asked, lifting her face for his kiss, when he rose to greet her.

"No, I'm early." Ever the perfect gentleman, he waited until she made herself comfortable on the plush velvet banquette, before reclaiming his own seat.

"What, no last minute emergencies?" She laughed, happy to be with him. Happy that he'd made the effort not to keep her waiting on her birthday. So often, he was delayed, or called away in the middle of whatever they'd planned, be it dinner, the theater, or making love. So often, he seemed preoccupied, distant, tense. Lately he'd even paced the floor some nights, then ended up sleeping in the guest room, worried he'd disturb her with his restlessness. She supposed that was the price a wife paid for being married to such a dedicated, sought-after cardio-thoracic surgeon.

"Not tonight," he said. "Ed Johnson's covering for me." He took the bottle of champagne, filled their flutes two-thirds full and raised his in a toast. "Happy birthday, Diana!"

"Thank you, sweetheart." The wine danced over her tongue, light and vivacious. Not too many years ago, the best they could afford when it came to celebrating special occasions was a bottle of cheap red wine and home-cooked spaghetti. Now, the only things red at the table were the long-stemmed roses, and there was nothing cheap about them.

Lifting the damp, sweet-smelling petals to her face, she eyed her husband mischievously. "These *are* for me, aren't they?"

"Those, and this, too." He pushed the foil-wrapped box toward her. "Open it before you order, Diana. I think you'll like it."

What was there not to like about a diamond and sapphire bracelet set in platinum? Speechless with pleasure, she fastened the lobster-claw clasp around her wrist, then tilted her hand this way and that, admiring the way the lamplight caught the fire and flash of the gems. "It's the most beautiful thing I've ever owned," she murmured, when she could speak. "Oh, Harvey, you've really gone overboard, this year. How am I supposed to compete with something like this, when *your* birthday comes around?"

"You won't have to." He smiled and gestured to the leather-bound menu in front of her. "What do you fancy for dinner?"

She studied the list of entrées. "I'm torn between the rack of lamb and the Maine lobster."

"Have the lobster," he urged. "You know it's your favorite."

"Then I will. With a small salad to start."

He nodded to the waiter hovering discreetly in the back-ground. "My wife will have the mesclun salad with lemon vin-aigrette, followed by the broiled lobster."

"And you, sir?" The waiter paused, eyebrows raised inquiringly.

Harvey lightly tapped the rim of his champagne flute. "I'm happy with the wine, thanks."

"You're not going to eat?" Perplexed, Diana stared at him. "Why not, sweetheart? Aren't you feeling well?"

"Never felt better," he assured her, reaching into his inside jacket pocket and pulling out a credit card. "The thing is, Diana, I'm leaving you."

Why a chill raced up her spine just then, she had no idea. But in less time than it took to blink, all her warm fuzzy pleasure in the moment, in the evening, evaporated. Striving to ignore it, she said, "You mean, you're going back to the hospital? But I thought you—?"

"No. I'm leaving you."

Still not understanding, she said, "Leaving me where? Here?"

"Leaving you, period. Leaving the marriage."

Heaven help her, she laughed. "Oh, honestly, Harvey! For a minute there, I almost believed you."

There was no answering smile on his face. Rather, pity laced with just a hint of contempt. "This is no joke. And before you ask why, I might as well tell you. I've met someone else."

"Another woman?" Her voice seemed to come from very far away.

"Well, hardly another man!"

"I suppose not." Very precisely, she set her champagne glass on the table, careful not to spill a drop. "And this woman…how long…?"

"Quite some time."

When she was six, she'd fallen into the deep end of her family's swimming pool and would have drowned if her father hadn't been close by and promptly hauled her to safety. Even so, she'd never forgotten the soundless, suffocating sensation that had briefly possessed her. Twenty-two years later, it gripped her again.

Floundering to find a lifeline in a world suddenly turned upside-down, she blurted, "But it won't last. These things never do. You'll get over it, over *her*…and I'll get past the hurt…I will, I promise! We'll pick up the pieces and go on, because that's what married people do. They honor their wedding vows."

He reached across the table, took both her hands firmly in his and gave them a shake. "Listen to me, Diana! This isn't a passing affair. Rita and I are deeply in love. I am committed to a future with her."

"No…!" She struggled to pull herself free of his hold. To shut out his words, and the cool, clinical dispassion with which he uttered them. As if he were wielding a scalpel on a comatose patient. As if she were incapable of feeling the pain. "You're in love with *me*. You've said so, a hundred times."

"Not for a very long time now. Not for months."

"Well, I don't care!" Distress and shock sent her own voice rising half an octave. "I won't let you throw us away. I deserve better than that…we both do."

He released her hands and sat very erect in his chair, as though to put as much physical distance between himself and her as possible in that intimate little corner of that intimate little restaurant. "Stop making a spectacle of yourself!" he hissed.

She clamped her mouth shut, but inside, every part of her was weeping—every part but her eyes. For some reason, they remained dry and hot and disbelieving. Still clutching at straws, she said, "Then what's all this about? The champagne and roses and bracelet?"

"It's your birthday." He shrugged. "I'm not completely without affection for you, you know. I wanted to give you something memorable to mark the occasion."

"And you thought telling me our marriage is over wouldn't do it?"

He regarded her pityingly. "Oh, come now, Diana! I can't believe you're entirely surprised. You must have realized things between us weren't the same anymore—that something vital had died."

"No. I sensed a change in you, but I put it down to stress at the hospital." She looked at the roses, at the gleaming sterling cutlery, at the platinum wedding ring on her left hand, and finally, at the man she'd married almost eight years ago. Then she laughed again, a thin, hollow, scraping sound that clawed its way up from the depths of her lungs. "But then, they do say the wife's always the last to know, don't they?"

"I can see that you're shocked, but in time you'll realize that it's better we make a clean break and end matters now, rather than wait until things deteriorate to the point that we can't speak a civil word to one another."

"Better for you, perhaps."

"And for you, too, in the long run." He drained his glass, and pushed back his chair. Again like the perfect gentleman he prided himself on being, he bent and kissed her cheek. "Enjoy your lobster, my dear. Dinner's on me."

Then he made his way across the restaurant to where the pregnant woman waited. She rose to meet him. He put his arms around her, gave her a lingering kiss full on the mouth, then ushered her out of the restaurant as carefully, as tenderly, as if she were made of blown glass.

Pregnant…

The woman he was leaving her for was having the baby he'd refused to give his wife. And at that, something really did die in Diana…

CHAPTER ONE

4:00 p.m., June 12

AIX-EN-PROVENCE was stirring from its afternoon siesta as Diana eased her ancient rental car onto the road that would take her to Bellevue-sur-Lac, fifty-three miles northeast of the town limits.

Aix-en-Provence: a beautiful city, rich in history, culture and art. The city where, twenty-nine years ago, a seventeen-year-old French girl allowed an American couple in their late forties to adopt her out-of-wedlock baby.

The city where Diana had been born...

Bellevue-sur-Lac, the village where she'd been conceived...

The names, the facts, the minute clues, were etched so clearly in her memory, she could recite verbatim the letter she'd found in her father's study, after her parents' death, two years previously.

Admittedly her husband's desertion had pushed them to the back of her mind for a while. A thousand times or more in the weeks after he left, she questioned where she'd gone wrong. Asked herself what she could have done differently that might have saved her marriage. But in the end, she'd been forced to accept that there was nothing. Harvey had fallen out of love with her, made up his mind he wanted to spend the rest of his life with someone else and that was that. She was alone, and he was not.

Seven months, though, was long enough to mourn a man who'd proven himself unworthy of her tears, and just over a week ago, she'd awoken to the realization that, little by little, her despair had melted away. Without her quite knowing when or how, her resentment toward Harvey had lost its bitter edge and sunk into indifference. If anything, she was grateful to him because, in deserting her, he'd also set her free. For the *first* time in her life, she could do exactly as she pleased without worrying that she might upset the people closest to her.

Which was why she now found herself in the south of France, heading toward a tiny lakeside village surrounded by lavender fields, olive groves and vineyards; and where, if the gods were on her side, she'd rediscover herself, now that she'd been legally stripped of her title and status as Dr Harvey Reeves's dutiful but dull little wife.

"You can't possibly be serious!" Carol Brenner, one of the few friends who'd stuck by her after she found herself single again, had exclaimed, when she learned what Diana had planned.

"Why ever not?" she'd asked calmly.

"Because it's crazy, that's why! For Pete's sake, haven't you gone through enough in the last seven months, without adding this?"

Shrugging, she said, "Well, they do say that what doesn't kill you, makes you stronger."

Carol shoved aside her latte and leaned across the coffee shop's marble tabletop, the better to make her point. "I'm not convinced you *are* stronger. Quite frankly, Diana, you look like hell."

"Oh, please!" she said ruefully. "Stop beating about the bush and feel free to tell me what you really think!"

"I'm sorry, but it's true. You've lost so much weight, you could pass for a refugee from some third world country."

Diana could hardly argue with that. Once she no longer had to prepare elegant dinners for her husband, she sometimes hadn't bothered preparing any dinner at all. As for breakfast, she'd skipped it more often than not, too. Which left lunch—a sandwich if she had any appetite, otherwise a piece of fruit and a slice of cheese.

"You've been like a ship without an anchor, the way you've drifted through this last winter and spring, not seeming to know what day it was, half the time," Carol went on, really hitting her stride. "And now, out of the blue, you announce you're off to France on some wild-goose chase to find your biological mother?" She rolled her eyes. "You'll be telling me next, you're joining a nunnery!"

"It's not out of the blue," Diana said softly. "This is something I've wanted to do for years."

"Diana, the point I'm trying to make is that I'm one of your closest friends, and I didn't even know you were adopted."

"Because it's always been a closely guarded secret. I didn't know myself until I was eight, and even then, I found out by accident."

Obviously taken aback, Carol said, "Good God, who decided it should be kept secret?"

"My mother."

"Why? Adopting a child's nothing to be ashamed of."

"It wasn't shame, it was fear. Apparently mine was a private adoption, and although my father made sure the legalities were looked after, the arrangement wasn't exactly…conventional. Once my mother realized the secret was a secret no longer, things at our house were never the same again."

"How so?" Carol asked.

Diana had rested her elbow on the table and cupped her chin in her hand, the events of that long-ago day sufficiently softened by time that she'd been able to relate them quite composedly….

She'd raced home from school and gone straight to the sunroom where her mother always took afternoon tea. "Mommy," she burst out breathlessly, "what does 'adopted' mean?"

Even before then, she'd understood that her mother was, as their cleaning lady once put it, "fragile and given to spells," and she realized at once that in mentioning the word "adopted," she'd inadvertently trodden on forbidden territory. The Lapsang Souchong tea her mother favored slopped over the rim of its translucent porcelain cup and into the saucer. "Good heavens, Diana," she said faintly, pressing a pale hand to her heart, "whatever makes you ask such a question?"

Horrified at having brought on one of the dreaded "spells," Diana rushed to explain. "Well, today Merrilee Hampton was mad at me because I won the spelling bee, so at recess she threw my snack on the ground, so I told her she was stupid, so then she told me I'm adopted. And I told her it's not true, and she said it is, because her mother said so, and her mother doesn't tell lies."

"Dear God, someone should staple that woman's mouth shut!"

Happening to come into the sunroom at that precise moment, Diana's father had flung himself into a wicker chair across from her mother's and said cheerfully, "Who are you talking about, my dear, and why are you ready to string her up by the thumbs?"

"Mrs. Hampton," Diana had informed him, since her mother seemed bereft of words. "She told Merrilee that I'm adopted, but I'm not, am I, Daddy?"

She'd never forgotten the look her parents exchanged then, or the way her father had taken her on his lap and said gently, "Yes, you are, sweet pea."

"Oh!" Terribly afraid she'd contracted some kind of disease, she whispered, "Am I going to die?"

"Good heavens, no! All being adopted means is—"

"David, please!" her mother had interrupted, her voice sounding all funny and trembly. "We decided we'd never—"

"*You* decided, Bethany," he'd replied firmly. "If I'd had my way, we'd have dealt with this a long time ago, and our child would have learned the truth from us, instead of hearing it from someone else. But the cat's out of the bag now, and nothing you or I can do is going to stuff it back in again. And after all this time, it can hardly matter anyway."

Then he'd turned back to Diana, tugged playfully on her ponytail and smiled. "Being adopted means that although another lady gave birth to you, we were the lucky people who got to keep you."

Trying to fit together all the pieces of this strange and sudden puzzle, Diana said, "Does that mean I have two mommies?"

"In a way, yes."

"David!"

"But you're our daughter in every way that counts," he went on, ignoring her mother's moan of distress.

Still unable to grasp so foreign a concept, Diana said, "But who's my other mommy, and why doesn't she live with us?"

At that, her mother mewed pitifully.

"No one you know," her father said steadily. "She was too young to look after a baby, and so, because she knew we would love you just as much as she did, and take very good care of you, she gave you to us. After that, she went back to her home, and we brought you here to ours."

"Well, I can see why you'd want to learn more about this woman," Carol said, when Diana finished her story. "I guess it's natural enough to be curious about your roots, especially when they're shrouded in so much mystery. What I don't understand is why you waited this long to do something about it."

"Simple. Every time I brought up the subject, my mother took to her bed and stayed there for days. 'Why aren't we enough for you?' she'd cry. 'Haven't we loved you enough? Given you a lovely home, the best education, everything your heart desires? Why do you want to hurt us like this?'"

"Uh-oh!" Carol rolled her eyes again. "I realized she was a bit over the top temperamentally, but I'd no idea she stooped to that kind of emotional blackmail."

"She couldn't help herself," Diana said, old loyalties coming to the fore. "She was insecure—very unsure of herself. I don't know why, but she never seemed to believe she deserved to be loved for herself, and nothing I said could convince her that, as far as I was concerned, she and my father were my true parents and that I adored both of them. In her view, my wanting to know about my birth mother meant that she and my father had failed. So eventually I stopped asking questions, and we all went back to pretending the subject had never arisen. But I never stopped wanting to find answers."

"Then tell me this. If it was that important to you, why didn't you pursue the matter after she and your father died, instead of waiting until now?"

"Harvey didn't think it was a good idea."

"Why ever not?"

"I think he was…embarrassed."

"Because you were adopted?"

"Pretty much, yes."

Carol made no effort to disguise her scorn for the man. "What was his problem? That you might not be blue-blooded enough for him?"

"You guessed it! 'You're better off not knowing,' he used to say, whenever I brought up the subject of my biological mother. 'She was probably sleeping around and didn't even know for sure who the father was. You could be anybody's brat.'"

"And you let him get away with that kind of crap?" Carol gave an unladylike snort. "You should be ashamed, Diana, that you let him walk all over you like that!"

"At the time, what mattered most was my marriage. I wanted it to succeed, and Harvey was under enough stress at the hospital, without my bringing more into our private life, as well."

"A fat lot of good it did you, in the end! He walked out anyway, and left you an emotional wreck."

"For a while, perhaps, but I'm better now. Stronger, in some ways, than I've ever been."

"Enough to stand the disappointment, if you don't find what you're looking for?"

"Absolutely," Diana said, and at the time, it had been true.

The car coughed alarmingly and clunked to a halt at the foot of a hill. *It serves you right,* Carol would have said. *If you'd taken the time to book ahead, you wouldn't have been stuck with an old beater of a car no right-minded tourist would look at.*

With some coaxing, she got the poor old thing running again, but as she approached a fork in the road, and found a sign pointing to the left, showing Bellevue-sur-Lac 31 kms, panic overwhelmed her and, for a moment, she considered turning to the right and heading for Monaco and a week of reckless betting on the roulette wheel, rather than pursuing the gamble she'd undertaken.

What if Carol was right, and she was inviting nothing but heartache for everyone by chasing her dream?

"The chances of your finding this woman are slim to non-existent, you know," her friend had warned. "People move around a lot, in this day and age. And even if you *do* find her, what then? You can't just explode onto the scene and announce yourself as her long-lost daughter. You could blow her entire life apart if she's married and hasn't confided in her husband."

"I realize that. But what's to stop me talking to her, or even to people who know her, and trying to learn a little bit about her? I might have half brothers or sisters, aunts and uncles. Grandparents, even. She was seventeen when she had me, which means she's only forty-five now. I could have a whole slew of relatives waiting to be discovered."

"And how will that help you, if they don't know who *you* are?" Carol asked gently.

It had taken all her courage to admit, "At least I'll know I'm connected to someone in the world."

"You have me, Diana. We might not share the same blood, but you're like a sister to me."

"You're my dearest friend, and I'd trust you with my life, which is why I'm confiding in you now," she replied. "But first and foremost, you're Tim's wife and Annie's mother." She opened her hands, pleadingly. "Can you understand what I'm saying?"

"Yes," Carol said, and her eyes were full of tears suddenly. "But I care too much about you to want to see you suffer another disappointment. You give your heart so willingly, Diana, and sometimes people see that as an invitation to trample all over it. Hotshot Harvey's done enough damage. Please don't leave yourself open to more. Don't let anyone take advantage of your generosity. Just once, think of yourself first, and others second."

The advice came back to her now as the car rattled around another bend in the road, and crossed a little stone bridge above a wide stream that burbled over brown rocks. Bellevue-sur-Lac 25 kms, a sign said.

What if she found her birth mother destitute? Abandoned by her family for her adolescent indiscretion? How could any decent person not lift a finger to help?

"I'll find a way," Diana promised herself, thumping the steering wheel with her fist. "I'll buy her a house, clothes, food—whatever she needs—and donate them anonymously, if I must."

It was the least she could do, if she was to live with herself, and heaven knew, she could afford it. Within reason, she could afford just about anything money could buy. In his eagerness to be rid of her and married to his mistress before the birth of their child, Harvey had been generous. Added to what she'd inherited from her parents, it added up to a very tidy sum. But would it be enough?

Probably not, she thought. When all was said and done, money never could buy the things that really mattered.

The car wheezed around another bend in the road. In the distance, she saw tidy rows of grapevines climbing a steep hillside. In the valley below, a subdued purple touched the earth. Lavender fields just bursting into bloom.

Another sign post, painted blue with white lettering. Bellevue-sur-Lac 11 kms.

Hand suddenly clammy with sweat, Diana eased the car over to the side of the road and rolled down the window. Wildflowers grew in the ditch, filling the air with their scent.

"Let me come with you," Carol had begged. "At least you'll have me in your corner if things don't go well."

Why hadn't she taken her up on the offer?

Because this was something she had to do by herself, that's why.

Reaching into her travel bag, she pulled out the single sheet of stationery she'd hoarded for so long. Spreading it over her lap, she smoothed out the creases, searching as she had so often in the past for any clues she might have missed that would help her now. The ink was faded, the script elegant and distinctly European.

Aix-en-Provence
December 10

Dear Professor Christie,
I write to inform you that Mlle. Molyneux has returned to her native village of Bellevue-sur-Lac. From all accounts, she appears to have put behind her the unhappy events of this past year, the nature of which she has kept a closely guarded secret from all who know her. I hope this will ease any concern you have that she might change her mind about placing her baby with you and your wife, or in any other way jeopardize the adoption.

I trust you are well settled in your home in the United States again. Once more, I thank you for the contributions you made to our university program during your exchange year with us.

With very best wishes to you, your wife and your new daughter for a most happy Christmas,
Alexandre Castongués, Dean
Faculty of Law
University Aix-Marseille

Did Mlle. Molyneux ever regret giving up her baby? Wonder if her little girl was happy, healthy? Or was she so relieved to be rid of her that she never wanted to be reminded of her, ever again?

There was only one way to find out.

Refolding the letter and stuffing it back in the side pocket of her travel bag, Diana coaxed the car to sputtering life again, shifted into gear and resumed her journey. Seven minutes later, the silhouette of a château perched on a cliff loomed dark against the evening sky. Immediately ahead, clustered along the shores of a long, narrow lake, buildings emerged from the dusk of early evening, their reflected pinpricks of light glowing yellow in the calm surface of the water.

Passing under an ancient stone arch, she drove into the center of the little village.

Bellevue-sur-Lac, the end of her journey.

Or, if she was lucky, perhaps just the beginning?

CHAPTER TWO

CROSSING the square en route to his car, which he'd left in the inn's rear courtyard as usual when he'd spent the day with the supervisor of his lavender operation, Anton noticed the woman immediately. Strangers who lingered in Bellevue-sur-Lac after sunset were a rarity, even during the summer months when travelers flocked to Provence. Usually they came for the day only, arriving early by the busload to tour the château, winery, lavender distillery and olive mills.

By now—it was almost half-past five o'clock—they were gone, not only because accommodation in the village was limited to what L'Auberge d'Olivier had to offer, but because they preferred the livelier nightlife in Nice or Marseille or Monaco.

This woman, though, sat at a table under the shade of the plane trees, sipping a glass of wine, and what captured his attention was not so much her delicate features and exquisite clothing, but her watchfulness. Her gaze scanned the passing scene repeatedly, taking note of every person who crossed her line of vision. At this moment, it was focused on him.

"Who's the visitor, Henri?" he asked, leaning casually against the outdoor bar where the innkeeper was busy polishing glasses in preparation for the locals, who'd gather later to drink cassis and play dominoes.

Henri paused in his task long enough to shoot an appreciative glance her way. "An American. She arrived last night."

"She'd reserved a room here?"

"No, she just showed up unannounced and asked if I could accommodate her. She's lucky the man you were expecting canceled at the last minute, or I'd have had to turn her away. Too bad he broke his leg, eh?"

"For him, and me both. I'm going to have to find someone to replace him pretty quickly." Again, Anton looked at the woman, observing her from the corner of his eye. Not just watchful, he decided, but nervous, too. Drumming her fingers lightly on the tabletop as if she were playing the piano. Keeping time by tapping her foot on the dusty paving stones. "What do you know about *her,* Henri?"

The innkeeper shrugged. "Not much. She speaks very good French, the high society kind. And she's in no hurry to leave here. She's taken the room for a month."

"A *month?*"

"That's what she said."

"Did she happen to mention why?"

"She did not."

When Marie-Louise died, reporters had descended on the area within hours, posing as innocent tourists to disguise the fact they were sniffing out scandal, real or imagined, with which to titillate their readers. In less than a week, Anton had been front-page news throughout France and most of Europe. *COMTE'S WIFE'S MYSTERIOUS DEATH,* the tabloid headlines screamed. *MURDER OR SUICIDE? POLICE QUESTION HUSBAND.*

Although public appetite for sensationalism eventually found other victims on which to feed, having his private life exposed to malicious speculation had been a nightmare while it lasted, not just for him and his immediate family, but for everyone in Bellevue-sur-Lac. Since then, he'd been mistrustful of strangers who chose to linger in such a backwater village, content to live in a small inn where they'd be sharing a common bathroom with other guests. And with the third anniversary of his wife's death coming up, he was especially wary. Like those which had gone before, it promised a burst of renewed interest in the whole tragic mess.

"One has to wonder how she plans to occupy her time," he remarked.

"Perhaps she's an artist."

She, and a hundred thousand others—would-be Cézannes, Van Goghs, Picassos, sure if they breathed the golden light of Provence, genius would ooze from their pores. They came looking suitably tormented by their muse, right down to their disheveled appearance and the paint under their fingernails.

Not this woman, though. She wouldn't allow a speck of dust to settle on her shoe.

Anton did not, as a rule, patronize the inn. Tonight, though, he was inclined to make an exception. He couldn't put his finger on exactly what it was, but something about the woman—the set of her slender shoulders, perhaps, or the tilt of her head—seemed vaguely familiar. That alone was enough to increase his suspicions. Had he seen her before? Was she one of the rabid reporters, come back for another helping of empty speculation?

"Pour two glasses of whatever the lady is drinking, Henri," he said, arriving at a decision.

Although Henri knew better than to say so, his face betrayed his surprise. Much might have changed since feudal times, but the people of Bellevue-sur-Lac and the surrounding area had been under the protection of the de Valois family for centuries. Whether or not he liked it, Anton reigned as their present-day *seigneur.*

They came to him to arbitrate their differences, to seek his advice, to request his help. That Monsieur le Comte would choose to sit among them at the L'Auberge d'Olivier, drinking the same wine they drank, would do more for Henri's reputation than if he'd been awarded the Legion of Honor.

As far as Anton was concerned, being the object of such reverence was nothing short of ludicrous. When all was said and done, he was just a man, no more able than any other to control fate. His wife's death and the reason behind it was proof enough of that. But tragedy and scandal hadn't been enough to topple him from his pedestal, any more than his disdain for his title relieved him of the obligations inherent in it.

"I should serve it immediately, Anton?" Henri wanted to know, still flushed with pleasure.

"No," he said, turning away. "I'll signal when we're ready."

The square was deserted now. No faces for the stranger to scrutinize. Instead she stared at her hands where they rested on the table.

"A beautiful woman should not sit alone on such a night, with only an empty glass for company," he said, approaching her. "May I join you?"

Startled, she looked up. Her face was a pale oval in the gloom, and he couldn't tell the color of her eyes, only that they were large. He'd addressed her in English, and she replied in kind. "Oh, no…thank you, but no."

It was his turn to be taken aback. Her slightly panicked rejection smacked more of propriety than guile. Hardly the response of a seasoned scandal-hunter, he thought. Or else, she was very good at hiding her true identity.

Covering his surprise with a smile, he said, "Because we haven't been formally introduced?"

She spared him the barest smile in return. "Well, since you put it that way, yes."

"Then allow me to rectify the matter. My name is Anton de Valois, and I am well-known in these parts. Ask anyone. They will vouch for me."

He thought she blushed then—another surprise—though it was hard to be sure, with night closing in. "I didn't mean to insult you," she said. She had a low, musical voice, refined and quite charming.

"Nor did you. It pays to be cautious these days, especially for a woman traveling by herself." Then, even though he already knew the answer, he paused just long enough to give his question the ring of authenticity before suggesting, "Or perhaps I'm mistaken and you're not alone after all, but waiting for someone else. Your husband, perhaps?"

"No," she replied, far too quickly, and lowered her eyes to stare at her left hand which was bare of rings. The lights in the square came on at that moment, glimmering through the branches of the plane tree to cast the shadow of her lashes in perfect dusky crescents across her cheeks. "No husband. Not anymore."

Again, not quite the attitude or the response he expected. Rather, she seemed lost, and very unsure of herself. On the other hand, he knew well enough that appearances could be deceiving. That being so, he led into the subject she'd surely latch on to with a vengeance, if she was indeed, as he suspected, a brash journalist with a hidden agenda.

"Then we share something of significance in common," he remarked, sliding into the chair across from hers without asking permission this time. "I also lost my spouse several years ago."

"Oh, I'm not a widow!" she exclaimed, meeting his gaze again. "I'm…divorced."

She uttered the word as if it were something of which she was deeply ashamed. A clever ploy, perhaps, designed to deflect attention from her true motives.

"What kind of man would be fool enough to let you go?" he inquired, sickened by the taste of false sympathy on his tongue. He was normally a straightforward man with little use for subterfuge.

"Actually…" She gave a tiny shrug and bit down briefly on

her lower lip. She had a very lovely mouth, he noticed. Soft, sensitive, defenseless. "He's the one who left me."

Afraid that the longer he engaged in a game of cat and mouse with such a woman, the duller the sharp edge of his suspicions might grow, Anton observed her closely, willing himself to uncover artifice, but finding only sincerity. Was he overreacting? At the mercy of his own paranoia—and she its innocent victim?

Suddenly despising himself for toying with memories she clearly found painful, he murmured with honest compassion, "In that case, he is a double fool and a cad. I can see that he's caused you much unhappiness."

"At the time, yes, but I'm over it now."

"And over him?"

She managed another smile, and if it was a trifle hesitant, it was also unmistakably genuine. "Oh, yes. Most definitely over him."

Choosing not to examine the real cause of the relief flooding through him, he nodded to Henri, who scooped up a tray bearing the two glasses of wine and a lighted candle, and brought it to the table. "Then we shall celebrate your freedom with a toast."

"No," she began. "It's very kind of you, but I meant what I said before. I really—"

Sweeping aside her objection, Anton said, "Henri, your lovely guest isn't certain it's safe to get to know me. Reassure her, will you, that I'm quite respectable?"

He'd switched to French, aware that Henri's English was minimal, at best. Without waiting for Henri to reply, she spoke, also in French, and it was, as the man had said, flawless. "I'm sure you're respectable enough. I'm just not accustomed to being approached by strange men."

"Strange men?" Henri set down the tray with a distinct thump. "Madame, you speak of the Comte de Valois!"

"A real live Comte?" She tipped her head to one side and this time managed a slight laugh. "In this day and age?"

Henri drew himself up to his full one hundred and seventy-five centimeters—about five feet eight inches in her part of the world. "A gentleman remains a gentleman, regardless of the times, Madame, and you may rest assured Monsieur le Comte fits the description in every way."

"Thanks, Henri," Anton intervened, knowing he scarcely deserved the accolade in the present circumstances. "That'll be all, for now."

She watched the innkeeper march back to the bar, his spine stiff with outrage, then switched her gaze to Anton again. "He wasn't joking, was he? You really are you a Count."

"I'm afraid so."

"Oh, dear! Then I owe you an apology. You must think me incredibly rude, not to mention gauche."

"I find you quite delightful," he said, and with the sense of floundering ever deeper into dangerous waters, realized he spoke the truth.

She clasped both hands to her cheeks. "I don't quite know how to behave or what to say. I've never had drinks with royalty before."

"I don't consider myself royalty. As for how you should behave, simply be yourself and speak your mind freely. Isn't that always the best way?"

"I'm not sure," she said. "It hasn't done me a lot of good, in the past."

He touched the rim of his glass to hers. "Then let us drink to the future. *À votre santé.*"

"*À votre santé aussi, Monsieur le Comte.*"

Continuing in French, he said, "To my friends, I am Anton."

"I hardly think I qualify as a friend on such short acquaintance."

The candle flame illuminated the classic oval of her face, the dimples beside her cupid's bow mouth and the delicate winged brows showcasing her eyes which, he saw now, were the same deep, intense blue as a Provencal sky in high summer. Her shoulder-length hair, worn simply, shone with the luster of a newly polished, old gold coin.

Was she beautiful?

Not in the conventional sense, no, he decided. Hers was a more subtle appeal, one he found quite irresistible. "Sometimes," he said earnestly, "friendship, like love, can strike instantly, as I believe it has between you and me."

"How can that be? You don't even know my name."

Returning her smile, he said, "You think I haven't noticed? I've been trying to learn it from the moment I saw you, but you've evaded me at every turn."

"It's no secret. I'm Diana. Diana…Reeves."

He noticed her slight hesitation, but decided not to push the point. She was skittish enough as it was. Instead, taking her hand, he raised it to his lips. "I'm very pleased to meet you, Diana Reeves. What did you have for dinner, last night?"

"Beef stew with potato dumplings."

"Then we'll order something different, tonight."

"I don't recall saying I'd have dinner with you. Not that that seems to mean much," she added ruefully. "I didn't agree to have a drink with you, either, but I'm doing it anyway. Do you always get your own way?"

"If I want something badly enough, I do. It's one of the perks of being a Count."

She regarded him soberly. "You're being very charming, Anton, and I'm sure most women would be flattered by your attention, but I think it's only fair to tell you that I'm not very good at flirting."

"I know," he said. "It's one of the qualities about you that I find most attractive."

"My ex-husband said I took things far too seriously and didn't know how to have fun."

"I thought we already established that your ex-husband is a fool."

Her dimples deepened as another smile lit up her face. "You're right, we did."

"Then forget about him and concentrate on us and friend-ship at first sight. When did you arrive in France?"

"Just yesterday."

"And you came straight here, to Bellevue-sur-Lac?"

At his question, tension emanated from her, so fierce that he half expected to see blue sparks crackling from the ends of her hair. "As a matter of fact, I did. What's wrong with that?"

Why so defensive, all of a sudden? he wondered, his suspi-cions on high alert again. "I didn't say there was anything wrong, Diana," he replied mildly.

Color swept into her cheeks. "Well, you *sounded* as if you did."

"Perhaps you interpreted surprise as disapproval."

"Why should you be surprised?"

He shrugged. "Bellevue-sur-Lac is barely a dot on the map of Provence, and has little to offer a tourist, yet you chose it over the many other, more interesting villages in the region."

Avoiding his glance, she said, "You might not think it inter-esting, but I find it thoroughly delightful."

"And on behalf of everyone living here, I thank you. But how did you discover it?"

She took a moment to consider her answer. "By chance," she said finally. "I'd fallen into a rut after my marriage ended, and decided I was ready for a little adventure. I knew I wanted to visit the south of France, so I stuck a pin on the map, promised myself I'd explore the spot I found, no matter what, and here I am. I consider myself lucky that I ended up in a place that offers food and lodging, and not on top of a mountain with nothing but the stars for company."

"Yet you're wasting the opportunity to see the best Provence has to offer. Why else do you think we make no real effort to accommodate tourists here?"

"I'm not exactly your average tourist. I don't care about seeing the sights. I just want a place where I can find a little peace."

A plausible enough story on the surface, and one he might

have accepted were it not that she still couldn't quite meet his gaze. "Not nearly as lucky as I consider myself, that you chose here," he returned smoothly. "Fate brought us together, no question about it, which means we definitely must dine together. I highly recommend Henri's bouillabaisse."

But she'd already gathered up her straw handbag and was preparing to leave. "Some other time, perhaps, but not tonight, thank you. After my earlier faux-pas, I'm afraid Henri might poison me. I even wonder if he'll still allow me to stay here."

A pity he couldn't keep her a little longer and discover the reason for her sudden uneasiness, Anton thought, but he had a whole month in which to uncover her secrets, and could afford to bide his time. "I don't think you need to concern yourself about that," he said, coming around the table to pull out her chair. "Henri Molyneux is one of the most equable fellows you'll ever meet."

In her eagerness to escape him, she must have risen too quickly because she staggered, and if he hadn't steadied her with a hand at her shoulder, he thought she might have fallen. As it was, her bag slipped from her grasp and fell on the table, knocking over her wineglass and sending it rolling to the dusty paving stones where it shattered.

Concerned, he said, "Diana? Are you okay?"

"No," she muttered distractedly, as breathless as if she'd run five kilometers in under five minutes. "I spilled my wine and broke the glass."

"*Alors,* don't worry about that. It happens all the time. See, Henri's already coming to clean it up."

"No," she insisted. "It's my mess. I'll clean it up."

Pressing her down onto the chair again, he said firmly, "You'll do no such thing. You're shaking, and white as a sheet. What's the matter?"

"*Nothing!*" she cried. Then, as if she realized she was behaving oddly, she made a concerted effort to pull herself together. "I'm sorry, I didn't mean to shout. It's just that I haven't eaten all day, and two glasses of wine on an empty stomach…"

"That settles it, then. We're having dinner." He nodded to Henri who, having shoveled up the broken glass, was wiping down the table. "How's the bouillabaisse coming along, my friend?"

"Not ready for another fifteen minutes, I regret to say," he replied, and cast an anxious glance at Diana. "You did not cut yourself, *madame?* You are not hurt?"

Diana stared at him wordlessly, her eyes huge. Two bright spots of color bloomed in her cheeks, making the rest of her face that much paler by comparison. Although the evening was pleasantly warm, she shivered as if it was winter and the mistral blew.

Baffled, Henri swung his glance to Anton. "Perhaps a little cognac might help?"

Equally mystified, Anton shook his head. There was more going on here than a missed meal. He was no doctor, but he recognized shock when he saw it. What he couldn't determine was its cause. In fact, nothing about this woman quite added up. "No alcohol," he said, laying his hand against her forehead and finding it clammy. "She's cold. Bring her a *tisane* and some bread instead."

She flinched at his touch, as if she'd been startled from sleep. "I don't need tea," she mumbled, struggling to her feet. "I'll get a sweater from my room."

"Send someone else for it. Those stairs—"

"No. I felt a little faint for a moment, but I'm fine now, and I'll be even better after I've freshened up a little."

"Very well," he conceded. "But don't think for a minute I'll allow you to miss dinner. If you're not back down here by the time the bouillabaisse is ready, I'm coming up to get you."

She managed a smile, as if the very idea of trying to avoid him would never cross her mind, and turned to Henri. "Fifteen minutes, you said?"

"At the very most, *madame.*"

"Okay. I'll be ready and waiting."

* * *

Yesterday, when the chambermaid had shown her to her room, Diana had considered it barely acceptable. At little more than twelve feet square, with its old, mismatched furnishings, it was, without question, the least sophisticated space she'd ever occupied, and certainly not one in which she planned to spend much time. Now, leaning against the closed door, she surveyed the narrow, iron-framed bed, hand-painted night table, carved armoire and three-drawer chest, with fond gratitude for the haven they represented.

Even the age-spotted mirror hanging above the old-fashioned washstand held a certain charm. Its most grievous sin lay in distorting her reflection on its wavy surface so that one half of her face looked as if it didn't quite belong to the other. Unlike Comte Anton de Valois, who possessed an unnerving talent for seeing clear through to her brain and detecting every nuance of hesitation, every carefully phrased falsehood.

She doubted he'd swallowed her excuse that hunger had left her light-headed, but it had been the best she could come up with on short notice, most especially since she really had been thrown for a loop at learning that Henri was a Molyneux.

"You are alone?" he'd inquired, when she'd shown up last night and requested a room.

She'd nodded and murmured assent, so captivated by every-thing she saw that it simply hadn't occurred to her to ask his full name. It had been enough that everyone called him Henri.

Bathing her in a welcoming smile, he'd pushed an old-fashioned ledger across the counter for her to sign. "Then you're in luck. It so happens a single room just became available."

L'Auberge d'Olivier was a picturesque building with the date, 1712, stamped above the open front door. Its thick plaster walls were painted a soft creamy-yellow. Flowers tumbled from baskets perched on the sills of its sparkling, deep-set windows. Outside, under a huge plane tree, candles flickered on wrought-iron tables where old men hunched over glasses of dark wine and smoked pungent cigarettes.

Charmed, she'd seen it as a fortuitous start to her search. Because Bellevue-sur-Lac was so small, she'd thought it would be easy to unearth clues that would lead her to her birth mother. Had spent this entire day combing the narrow streets, convinced success was around the next corner. Behind the protection of her sunglasses, she'd scrutinized every woman she came across, searching for a physical resemblance, a visceral intuition, that would tell her she'd found the right one. But the very smallness of the village turned out to be a serious drawback.

"How do you plan to tackle this harebrained scheme of yours?" Carol had asked, just before she'd dropped her off at SeaTac airport.

"Very discreetly," Diana had replied smugly. "I'll be so smooth and subtle, no one will even notice me, let alone guess what I'm after."

In fact, she'd been an object of suspicious curiosity everywhere she went. Although they'd been polite enough, people had closed ranks against her, not trusting a lone American wandering the area, and she'd come back to the inn that evening, no farther ahead than she had been when she'd left there that morning.

Was she really so naive that she'd expected all she had to do was show up, and her mother would instinctively know her? So foolish as to think that, in the unlikely event such a miracle occurred, a woman who'd kept her baby's birth a secret for over twenty-eight years would willingly reveal it now?

"You're rushing into this, Diana," Carol had warned. "You need to take a step back and consider the pitfalls, the most obvious being that you're the world's worst liar. What makes you think you can pull off such a monumental deception?"

She should have listened to her friend. Perhaps then, she wouldn't have made a spectacle of herself with a man smart enough to recognize something fishy when it was staring him in the face.

And so accustomed to having his own way that he wouldn't take "no" for an answer.

What had he threatened, before she fled to the sanctuary of her room? *Be down here by the time the bouillabaisse is ready, or I'm coming up to get you,* or words to that effect?

That he meant it was enough to have her changed into fresh clothes and on her way downstairs again in record time. If there was to be a confrontation, better it take place in public, than here in a room that was barely large enough for one. He was too pushy, too sure of himself—and, she admitted reluctantly, altogether too attractive for her to deal with him at close quarters.

She needed to keep her wits about her because, just when she'd been ready to concede defeat and admit Carol had been right all along, the one lead she'd hoped to find had fallen almost literally into her lap. Henri Molyneux, her host, might very well be the key to the mystery of who her birth mother was, and whether or not he knew it, Anton de Valois was going to help Diana unlock it.

Falling under his charming spell would undermine her resolve and might very well turn out to be a fatal mistake, because he struck her as a man of many layers; a classic example of the old saying that still waters run deep.

She must resist him at all costs.

CHAPTER THREE

A MAN likes to be seen with a woman who knows how to dress, Harvey used to say. *That she cares enough about his opinion to want to make him proud when he takes her out in public, tells him he made the right choice in marrying her.*

A belittling definition of a wife's worth, Diana thought now, although she hadn't said so at the time, and she was pretty sure Anton de Valois would see past such superficiality. Even so, she dressed with care, and from the way his glance swept over her in frank approval when she joined him again, knew she'd chosen well. Her sleeveless navy dress, deceptively simple but superbly cut, was enhanced only by a silver bracelet, lending just the right touch of low-key elegance for what, to all apparent intents and purposes, was supposed to be a low-key dinner.

"You took rather longer to return than you were supposed to, but it was well worth the wait," he remarked, pulling out her chair. "You look quite lovely, Diana, and very much better than you did half an hour ago."

"Thank you. I'm feeling better." She took her seat, outwardly poised, but when his hand brushed against her bare skin, a shock of sensual heat flashed through her, and briefly— *very* briefly indeed!—she longed to lean into his touch and soak in his warmth.

This was a man put on earth to tempt a woman to stray from

her intended course. He turned her thoughts to such nonsense as love at first sight, to happy-ever-after, when any person with a grain of sense knew there was no such thing. Yet for all that she tried to distance herself from him, his magnetism tugged at her, drawing her ever deeper into its aura.

Simply put, she found him both irresistible and intriguing. The cast of his mouth, the slow-burning fire in his eyes, spoke of a passion which, once aroused, be it from anger, pride or sexual desire, would not easily be quenched. The lean strength of his body betrayed a working familiarity with manual labor, yet cashmere, silk and fine leather were created with his particular brand of natural elegance in mind.

Why hadn't she met him sooner, before she'd learned to be so wary, so disillusioned? she lamented. Before she'd married the wrong man and had all her womanly dreams turned to ashes?

Annoyed by her wandering thoughts, she stiffened her spine, both physically and mentally. She was here on a mission, and the handsome French Count resuming his seat across from her, merely the means to an end.

Blithely ignorant of her thoughts, the handsome French Count smiled winningly and said, "Enough to tolerate a glass of wine before we eat?"

"Perhaps not quite that much," she said, deciding she needed to keep a clear head. So what if his voice was dark as midnight, his smile enough to melt the polar ice cap, and his face the envy of angels? She'd learned the hard way how easily sexual awareness could cloud other important issues between a man and a woman, and she wasn't about to let it lead her astray again. "At least, not until I have some food in my stomach."

He indicated a basket containing a sliced baguette, and a shallow dish of black olives mashed to a paste with roasted garlic. "Try some of this, then. Henri bakes his own bread, and the olives are home grown on de Valois soil."

"Ah! So you own olive groves. I was wondering how Counts earn their keep these days."

She spoke lightly, hoping he wouldn't discern such a nakedly transparent attempt to discover more about him. But knowledge was power, and the more she learned about Anton de Valois, the better prepared she'd be to withstand his appeal and deal with whatever it was that really motivated his interest in her. Because all his smooth Continental charm notwithstanding, the alert calculation in his gaze whenever it settled on her, betrayed him. For some reason she couldn't begin to fathom, he didn't trust her. And *that,* she reminded herself sternly, was ample reason for her not to trust him.

"Olives keep me busy enough," he replied, bathing her in a singularly breathtaking smile, "but they're by no means my chief obsession."

She spread a little of the paste on a piece of bread and sampled it. "They should be. This is outstanding."

"Then I insist you try at least a mouthful of the wine. My vineyards produced the grapes which my vintner blended to create this very fine Château de Valois Rouge."

"Thanks anyway, but I'll take your word for it. As I mentioned not five minutes ago, I don't care for any wine right now."

She might as well have saved her breath. "*Mon dieu,* Diana, relax and live a little!" he scoffed, pouring a small amount into her glass. "A sip or two won't send you to hell in a hand cart, but I promise you, it will enhance your meal. In this part of Provence, a well-chilled red wine is, to bouillabaisse, what American beer is to pretzels."

It was a pretty wine, she had to give him that. It glowed in her glass with all the fire of a ruby. Still, if getting her drunk was his aim, he was in for a disappointment. She found him intoxicating enough, without falling victim to his *vin rouge.* She'd wet her lips with the stuff, and that was all.

"Very pleasant," she said, allowing a mere trickle to roll

down her throat, and changed the subject before he decided she hadn't tasted enough to know if it was wine or water. "So what else keeps you busy, apart from overseeing your vineyards and olive groves?"

"Doing the same for my lavender farm and distillery. I'm a hands-on kind of man and, given a choice, I'd prefer to be more actively involved in the actual operation of all three enterprises, but the administrative end of things is so time consuming that I frequently put in ten-hour days without once setting foot outside my office."

"My goodness, you really *are* a working model of a Count! What do you do for relaxation?"

She realized at once her mistake. Without missing a beat, he lowered his long lashes in seductive slow motion, a move that aroused a disturbing response in the pit of her stomach. "Coerce beautiful Americans into having dinner with me. Speaking of which, here comes our bouillabaisse. Prepare to be impressed."

Oh, she was already impressed, pathetically so, but not by Henri's culinary skills! Anton de Valois, however, was a different matter altogether. She should be ashamed for falling victim to the practiced moves of the French equivalent of Don Juan!

Henri arrived at their table, wheeling a cart holding a thick pottery tureen on a matching platter, as well as bowls, plates and cutlery. With great pomp and ceremony, he removed the tureen lid and wafted his hand over the escaping steam, sending a mouthwatering aroma of slow-simmered tomatoes, garlic, saffron and herbs drifting her way.

Chunks of red mullet, monkfish, John Dory and conger eel, as well as mussels and various other shellfish, floated in the rich broth. *"Bon appetit, mes amis!"* he pronounced with a smile, and left them to it.

Anton ladled a generous helping of the stew into a bowl and passed it to Diana. "Try this and tell me what you think," he coaxed.

What she privately thought was that simply feasting her eyes on him and drinking in his charm was sustenance enough. But since that route surely led to nothing but trouble, she wrenched her runaway emotions under control, obediently took a spoonful of the fish stew, savored it slowly, then closed her eyes and sighed with genuine pleasure. "Pure heaven!" she sighed.

"That's pretty much the reaction Henri Molyneux always gets when his bouillabaisse is on the menu."

She couldn't have asked for a better reminder of the *real* reason she was supposed to be sharing a meal with him. Swallowing her food along with the lie she was about to fabricate, she said, "I don't think I've come across that name before."

Another mistake she quickly came to regret! "A woman with your fluency in French has never heard the name *Henri?*" Anton inquired with blatant disbelief. "Come now, Diana! You surely don't expect me to swallow that!"

"Oh, not his *first* name," she amended hastily, a telltale blush warming her face. "I was referring to Molyneux. Is it…very unusual?"

"Not in these parts," he said, continuing to eye her suspiciously. "There are Molyneux's everywhere."

Her pulse gave an erratic leap. Struggling to sound as if she was merely making trivial dinner conversation when, in reality, her entire world hung on his reply, she asked lightly, "Don't tell me they're all related."

"Not necessarily all, but quite a few, certainly. So many families are linked, either directly, or through marriage. As I said, it's a very common name. Henri, for instance, is the eldest of seven children, and has three of his own, as well as two grandchildren."

"He doesn't look old enough to be a grandfather."

Anton rolled his rather magnificent eyes. "Tell him that, and he'll be your slave for life! He turns sixty next month. I know, because a big birthday bash is in the works, to which everyone within a fifty-mile radius is invited."

Filing away that gem of information, Diana continued her inquisition with a casual, "What about his siblings? Are they married, as well?"

"Yes, and all but one with children and grandchildren of their own. At last count, there were thirty-eight Molyneux's in his branch of the family alone. Multiply that a few times, and you'll understand why I say the name is as thick on the ground in these parts, as plane tree leaves in autumn."

Little pieces of her personal jigsaw puzzle were beginning to fall into place almost too neatly. Trying hard to contain her growing excitement, Diana said, "And Henri's six siblings, are they all brothers?"

"The youngest is a sister, and just as well, according to Henri's father. Gérard always said that if the seventh baby had been another boy, he'd have been kicked out of the house and made to spend the rest of his days with the cows in the barn. Not that anyone believed the story. He and his wife were devoted to each other, and to their sons. But from what I understand, there's no doubt that Jeanne was special. Their whole family adored her."

"Does she have children, too?"

"No," he said coolly. "Tell me, Diana, why are we talking about people who can't possibly be of interest to you, when we could be spending the time getting to know one another better?"

Back off! the voice of caution advised. *You're betraying too much interest in the Molyneux family and arousing his suspicion!* But increasingly convinced she was finally onto something, Diana ignored the warning and leaned forward urgently. "I don't agree. Even the lives of strangers are interesting, so please go on."

"Go on?" The chill in his voice was more pronounced than ever. "Go on with what, exactly?"

She needed to stop. To dismiss the subject with a laugh, and turn the conversation to something light and inconsequential.

And she would have, if it hadn't been that so much of what he told her fit the profile of her birth mother. Henri was almost sixty and the eldest of seven. He had only one sister, the baby of the family, and the woman Diana had traveled halfway around the world to find was forty-five. Mental arithmetic might never have been her strong point, but even she could do the math on this one.

"With what you were telling me about Henri's family," she said, hard-pressed not to reach across the table and literally shake the words out of him. "The whole idea of seven children in one family fascinates me."

"Really," he said, with marked skepticism.

"Yes, really!"

He regarded her steadfastly over the rim of his glass, and took a slow sip of his wine. "Then I'm sorry to disappoint you but there's nothing else to tell. The Molyneux's are good people, and that's about it."

He was wrong. One ambiguity remained, and terrified though she was of what she might learn if she questioned it, the prospect of remaining in ignorance terrified her even more. She'd lived with enough uncertainty to last her a lifetime. She wouldn't allow it to derail her now. So, clearing her throat, she plunged ahead. "But I notice you speak of Henri's sister in the past tense. Is that because she died?"

Oh, how horribly blunt the words sounded, and Anton must have thought so, too, because he almost choked on his bouillabaisse. *"Mon dieu, non!"* he exclaimed. "Why would you think such a thing?"

"I'm not sure," she said, fumbling for a plausible reply. "It was just the way you spoke of her, that's all. It made me feel…sad."

"But why? You don't even know these people. Why do you care about them?"

"I don't," she whispered, blinking furiously to stem the sudden rush of tears welling in her eyes.

But he was too observant to be so easily fooled. "That simply isn't true. Clearly you care very much—indeed, far more than the occasion warrants. Did my speaking of the Molyneux's somehow revive unhappy memories of your own family?"

The candle flame bloomed into a multihued disc, perforated at its rim with pinpricks of brilliance. She blinked to clear her vision and a tear rolled down her face. "In a way. Hearing you talk about families and marriage brought home to me that I don't have either anymore."

"Your parents—?"

"Died within six months of each other, two years ago."

"And you were an only child?"

I don't know for sure, she cried inwardly. *That's what I'm trying to find out.* "Yes."

"Then we have even more in common than I first supposed," he said, with more kindness and compassion than Harvey had ever shown, "because I, too, was an only child. My parents died in a train derailment when I was seven, and I was left in the care of my two aunts who live with me still."

"Oh, Anton!" she cried, mortified. "You must think I'm incredibly self-absorbed, to be wailing on about my own woes, when you had a much tougher time of it."

"Not at all. My aunts are exceptional people and came as close as anyone could to taking the place of my mother and father. Of course, I grieved, but I never felt alone or abandoned, because those two women, who never married or bore children of their own, stepped into the role of parents as naturally and wholeheartedly as if they'd been preparing for it their entire lives. They loved me unconditionally, gave me the gift of laughter, instilled in me a respect for others, taught me the meaning of integrity and never once lied to me."

He paused a moment, seeming lost in thought, then suddenly lifted his gaze and stared at Diana. The absolute candor in his eyes, the utter integrity shining through, struck her with such force that, with a sudden sense of shock, she found herself wishing *he'd* been the man she'd married.

Yes, he was a stranger, and yes, he made her uneasy with his probing gaze, but she knew instinctively that he'd never have cheated on her. Never have lied so cruelly.

"At the end of the day, they're the qualities that define us as human beings. Without them, we're not worth very much at all," he finished soberly. "Don't you agree?"

Shame flooded through her. How was she supposed to reply, knowing as she did that she was deliberately misleading him about herself and her reason for being there? Yet he was too astute not to notice if she tried to evade his question.

"In principle, yes," she finally allowed, steering as clear of outright deceit as possible. "Unfortunately no one's perfect, and even the best of us sometimes fall short."

He continued his close observation a few unnerving seconds longer, then dropped his gaze to her hands, playing nervously with the stem of her wineglass. "I appear to have a talent for making you uncomfortable, *ma chère*."

"Whatever makes you think that?"

"You keep fidgeting with your glass."

"Well, if you must know," she said, somehow managing to meet his unwavering gaze without flinching, "I think I might like a little more wine, after all."

"As you wish." He poured an inch into the bowl of her glass. "This is a Syrah and something of an experiment for us. Take a decent taste, this time, and save your dainty sipping for afternoon tea with English royalty."

Add "insufferably arrogant" to his list of qualities, she told herself, bristling at his tone, and just to let him know she wasn't a complete ignoramus, she took her time going through the ritual of sniffing, swirling and tasting the wine.

"Well?" he demanded imperiously. "Will it do?"

Still playing for time, she let the mouthful she'd taken linger on her tongue a moment longer, swallowed, then closed her eyes and did that weird little trick of exhaling down the back of her throat to catch a final bouquet—the mark of a true oenophile, according to Harvey, who'd always made an exorbitantly big deal of conferring approval on the wine, when they entertained or dined out.

"Delightfully complex, with a remarkable nose," she conceded.

Harvey would have been tickled pink by her performance. Anton, on the other hand, didn't seem at all impressed. He simply poured more wine into both their glasses and returned to a subject she'd hoped he'd forgotten about. "You mentioned earlier that you came here looking for a little peace."

"That's right."

"I've always seen peace as a state of mind, not a place on the map."

"Normally I'd agree with you, but I needed a change of scene, as well."

"Why is that?"

"Because running into my ex-husband all the time wasn't helping me recover from the breakup of my marriage."

"You live in a small town where that sort of thing happened often, do you?"

"No. I live in Seattle."

"Ah, the Space Needle city." He raised his elegant eyebrows derisively. "Large enough, I'd have thought, that you could easily avoid one another, unless, of course, you work together."

"Hardly! He's a surgeon."

"And what are you, Diana?" he inquired, imbuing the question with unspoken skepticism.

"Nothing," she said, rattled as much by his questions as the cool disbelief with which he received her answers. "I was his wife, and now I'm nothing. Why are you giving me the third degree like this?"

"Is that what I'm doing?"

"Well, what would *you* call it?"

"Getting to know you." He permitted himself a satisfied little smile and lifted his shoulders in a perfectly executed Continental shrug. "You surely can't blame me for that?"

He was playing with her the way a cat plays with a mouse before closing in for the kill. And she was helpless to put a stop to it.

Oh, he was too suave, too sure of himself, too…*everything,* with his chiseled features, and sexy, heavily lashed eyes, and tall, elegant frame! "How am I supposed to answer that, Anton?"

"You can start by relaxing, and not judging every man you meet by your former husband. As for your remark about being nothing, that's absurd. You're intelligent and beautiful and sensitive, three good reasons for any man with half a brain to find you interesting. How long do you plan to stay here?"

The man had the unnerving habit of infiltrating a woman's defenses then, before she could regroup, firing a sudden question in her face. "A few weeks," she admitted, bracing herself for further interrogation.

"Good. That means we can see more of each other."

"I'm not sure I'm ready to start dating again."

"I'm not casting myself in the role of suitor," he informed her dauntingly. "I'm extending the hand of friendship to a stranger, in an effort to ensure she leaves here satisfied that it was worth the time and effort it took her to make the journey in the first place."

Good grief, was the man *never* at a loss for just the right words? "I already feel that way."

"Excellent!" He added more wine to her glass. "So tell me, Diana, what were you, before you became a wife?"

"A university student, majoring in modern languages. I'd hoped to become a teacher after I graduated."

"But you changed your mind?"

"Yes."

"Because you decided you didn't like children enough to want to spend six or more hours a day with them, ten months of the year?"

"Not at all! I love children. If it had been up to me—" She stopped, Harvey's ultimate betrayal flaring up like a nagging toothache that never quite went away. "But it wasn't."

"You couldn't have children?" Anton asked, his voice hypnotizing in its sudden deep sympathy.

"I don't know, because I never tried. Harvey thought we should wait until he was established before we started a family, so I quit university and went to work as a translator for a law firm whose major clients were European."

"What you're saying, in a very nice way, is that you put your own career and wishes on hold, in order to promote your husband's."

"Something like that, yes."

"I wonder how long it will be before this foolish man realizes what a treasure he cast aside—which is, of course, exactly what will happen, in time."

"I rather doubt that."

Reaching across the table, he wrapped her fingers warmly in his in a way that gave her palpitations. "But if it did, and he asked, would you take him back?"

"Never," she managed breathlessly, and wondered what it was about him that left her feeling as if she'd never held hands with a man before.

Whatever the reason, she steeled herself to resist him. Because, of course, he *was* coming on to her, whether or not he admitted it, and given half a chance, he'd probably be quite happy to take her to bed and make love to her.

The problem was, although he'd probably dismiss such a happening as a pleasant summer interlude, she was an all-or-nothing kind of woman, no better at casual sex than she was at flirting. Emotionally vulnerable and needy as she knew herself to be, she couldn't afford to lay her heart on the line again, just to have him trample all over it when he decided he'd had enough of her. She'd already gone through that with Harvey, and once was enough.

"That's what I was hoping to hear," Anton said, bathing her in a slow, seductive smile that threatened to reduce her rational judgment to a blob of molten hormones. "I'd hate to have to challenge him to a duel at dawn."

She untangled her fingers from his while she still retained a smidgeon of common sense. "There's no danger of that. My ex-husband is no more interested in me than I am in him."

"What does interest you, then?"

"Catching up on my sleep." She faked a yawn behind her hand. "It's past my bedtime."

He made a big production of looking at his watch. "You're surely not serious?"

"I surely am."

"But the night is still young, *ma belle ange.*"

Withstanding his flattery was definitely more than she could handle. "Not for me, it isn't," she insisted, forcing herself to her feet and clutching her purse to her breasts like a shield. "I'm fading fast, and your wine, excellent though it was, isn't helping any. Good night, Anton. Thank you for a lovely evening."

Before she could make the speedy exit she'd planned, he was on his feet and blocking her escape. "The pleasure was all mine," he murmured, brushing his lips over the back of her hand.

That she could deal with. He was French, after all, and a Count, to boot. But then, instead of releasing it, he turned her hand over and pressed a soft, warm kiss in the center of her palm. And for reasons that completely eluded her, she felt the effect all the way to the soles of her feet. She wasn't absolutely certain, but she thought she might even have let out a tiny whimper of pleasure, too.

Accurately guessing exactly the effect he'd had on her, he

folded her fingers over the spot, and fixed her in a gaze veiled by his fringe of dense black lashes drooping at half-mast. "Until tomorrow, Diana," he murmured.

Not if she had any say in the matter! Vividly aware of his gaze measuring her every step, she resisted the urge to bolt, and schooled herself to walk with a reasonable facsimile of decorum through the inn's front door. Then, when she was quite sure she was out of his sight, she *did* bolt, scuttling up the stairs and down the narrow corridor to the sanctuary of her little room as if the devil himself were in pursuit.

The woman was a mass of contradictions, he decided, watching as the light came on in her room. Educated, refined and with a certain sophistication, on the one hand; on the other, curiously naive and unsure of herself.

She blushed like a teenager, and looked out on the world with the eyes of an innocent. But she'd pursued her interest in Henri and his family with the sharp-minded tenacity of a terrier on a rat. If, as Anton had first suspected, she was really a tabloid reporter hiding behind a false identity, she was either very good at what she did, or hopelessly inept.

Instinct told him that she had a hidden agenda, and he'd learned long ago to trust his instincts. Yet despite his doubts and suspicions, he found himself drawn to her like no other woman he'd ever met. All of which made her doubly dangerous to his peace of mind.

Absorbed in his thoughts, he didn't notice his general manager had joined him until the man dropped into her recently vacated chair. Julien Laporte looked after the publicity end of things, and was very good at it. But from the discouraged slump of his shoulders now, he clearly brought bad news.

"I'm glad I caught you, Anton," he began. "That university student who was supposed to replace the other who broke his leg, has changed his mind and won't be coming to work for us this summer, after all. I've called in all my markers, trying to find a suitable substitute, and come up empty-handed. The kind of seasonal employee with the qualifications we're looking for was snapped up long ago. The way things look right now, we might be forced to cancel tours of the château and gardens this summer. A pity, I know, but better that than to bring in someone unable to do the job well. We have a reputation to maintain."

Up in her room, Diana showed no sign of her professed exhaustion as she paced back and forth in front of the window. Even from a distance, it was obvious she was either very agitated, very excited, or both.

"Courage, *mon ami!*" Anton replied thoughtfully, pushing himself to his feet. "We haven't exhausted all our options quite yet. Order us a cognac, Julien, and I'll be right back."

He could have made no secret of where he was going, and simply entered the inn through the main entrance and made his way upstairs in full view of the other patrons. But not even he would have been able to silence the gossip such a move would provoke, so in the interest of discretion, he went around the back of the building to where an iron fire escape connected the upper floor to the rear courtyard.

As usual at this time of year, the door at the top stood open, giving him easy access to the interior. What struck him as somewhat less usual was that her bedroom door also was slightly ajar. Not only that, her voice floated clearly into the quiet corridor, and given the frequent pauses in the conversation, it became immediately clear that she was on the phone.

"I was all ready to give up," he heard her say. "Honestly, Carol, it just seemed as if the entire village closed ranks against me…. Oh, no one actually *said* anything, but I could tell they were wondering what I was doing there…I know you said it wouldn't be easy, but I really thought I'd pick up some sort of lead that would point me in the right direction, since I could hardly just come straight out and ask… Oh, stop saying 'I told you so.' I can lie along with the best, when I have to, and do it without swallowing my tongue!

"...Okay, that's why I called you, because the day turned out not be a total loss after all. I met the local Count...yes, *that* kind, although I haven't noticed anyone tugging on a forelock when they address him. They're respectful enough, without going overboard.... How do I know? Because I ended up having dinner with him, that's how... In his mid-thirties, I'd guess...

"Well, now that you mention it, yes, he is. Rather too gorgeous, for my peace of mind. Reminds me a bit of George Clooney and I don't mind telling you, when I'm with him, I have a hard time focusing on why I'm here. Look, the point is, he's the one who gave me the opening I've been looking for, so first thing tomorrow, I'll follow up on it. Just think, Carol, the next time I call, I might have real news...

"I *am* being careful. I can see the square from my window. He's already left, and some other guy's at our table.... I know, I'm losing you, too. It's because I'm using my cell phone, instead of the public phone downstairs, and the reception's not the best.... Of *course* I'll keep you posted. Say hi to Tim, and sorry I disturbed you so early in the day, but I knew you'd be anxious to find out how things are going...."

So she was a fraud, just as he'd suspected! Stealthily Anton retraced his steps, fueled by a flame of anger that reduced his attraction to ashes. In its place rose a grim determination to best her at her own game.

Given a choice, he'd have her run out of town before she could put into action whatever plans had brought her here, but even the Comte de Valois couldn't resort to such extreme measures on the strength of eavesdropping. However, he'd learned at his father's knee the value of an iron fist disguised in a velvet glove when necessity called for one, and he'd have no compunction about using it in this instance.

Whatever she was up to, he'd uncover it, and the easiest way to accomplish that was by keeping her firmly in his sights. And from her unguarded comments to whoever Carol was, he knew exactly how to go about it.

Whether or not she was ready to admit it, Diana Reeves was starving for male attention, and ripe for the plucking. And he was more than man enough for the job.

Nobody made a fool of Anton de Valois with impunity, least of all a slip of a woman like her.

CHAPTER FOUR

"*Work* for you?" Diana almost blew coffee in his face.

It was seven-thirty, only. Early enough, she'd thought, that she could sit undisturbed in the morning sun, sipping café au lait from the huge bowl-shaped cup Henri had brought out to her. Then, before he became too busy with his regular customers, she'd hoped to engage him in casual conversation, to help her ferret out enough information about his sister to deduce whether or not she might indeed be Diana's mother. But within five minutes, Anton de Valois had shown up, plunked himself down at her table as if he owned it, and made the outrageous suggestion that she spend her time here acting as tour guide at his château.

"Don't think of it as work," he chided affably, looking disgracefully wide-awake and sexy in a narrow-striped, green and white shirt, and superbly tailored black pants. "Think of it as helping out a friend in need."

"We're not friends."

He regarded her from soulful, incredibly beautiful gray eyes. "You wound me. I thought we established, last night, that we are. What changed your mind?"

My good friend, Carol, she could have told him. *She quite rightly warned me to watch my step around you.* "Last night, the wine was talking. I'm seeing things in a different light, this morning."

"I dispute that. You drank almost nothing. But even if you're right, that's still no reason to turn me down without at least considering my proposal. I really am in a bind, *ma chère* Diana. I wouldn't have come to you, if I wasn't."

At the best of times, she'd never been much good at saying "no" to people, least of all someone as persistent and persuasive as the inestimable Count. Given the way she'd tossed restlessly most of the night, mostly because of him, this morning found her at an even greater disadvantage. "Why me?" she asked resentfully. "Corral one of the locals to help you out."

"I would, if I could, but for this particular job, it's simply not an option. To begin with, it's seasonal work only, and those living here who choose to work are already fully employed. That's why I usually hire university students, since they're always eager to make money over the summer. But just as important, I need someone completely fluent in English and French, and preferably with a working knowledge of Italian and Spanish, also." He sent her one of his winning smiles. "All of which, in the absence of a language arts student, makes you the ideal candidate. So, what do you say, Diana? Will you do it?"

"No."

"I'm prepared to pay you well for your time."

"I don't care about the money."

"Then what's the problem?"

"You are," she said bluntly. "Last night, you inflicted yourself on me, even though I made it clear I preferred to be alone, and you're doing it again now, before I've finished my first cup of coffee. Stop badgering me, Anton. I'm barely awake yet."

"You're not a morning person," he purred soothingly. "I understand. But that's the nice thing about this job. You don't have to be up at the crack of dawn. The tours don't start until eleven. You can sleep in as late as you like."

"In case I didn't make myself clear last night, I'm here on holiday."

"But, Diana," he said, trying hard to look guileless, and succeeding about as well as the wolf, right before it jumped out of bed and attacked Red Riding Hood, "how are you going to fill your days when there's nothing to do here but soak up the sun and watch the hours drift by?"

"After the year I've just had, the prospect of doing nothing but soak up the sun and watch the hours drift by, holds more appeal than you can possibly begin to appreciate." *And it's a whole lot safer than being around you all day!*

"For a little while, perhaps, but it'll lose its charm soon enough, and you'll wish you had something more stimulating to occupy your mind."

The problem, Anton, is that I find you altogether too stimulating—and not just in my mind!

Dousing the thought before it transposed itself into a betraying blush, she said staidly, "If that indeed happens, I'll be sure to let you know. Meanwhile, I plan to wade through the stack of books I brought with me, write letters to friends I haven't contacted in months, take lots of photographs as souvenirs of my travels, and soak up local color as well as sunshine. Trust me, that's stimulation enough."

"If you come to work for me, you'll still be able to do all those things," he cajoled.

"No," she said again, quickly, before her determination wavered. "Go away, and leave me alone. You might be able to bend everyone else in these parts to your will, but you're not going to railroad me."

As though realizing looking bereft and helpless wasn't helping his cause, Anton changed tactics. "It would seem I'm wasting my time," he declared loftily, lifting his shoulders in one of his trademark shrugs. "If your idea of saturating yourself in local custom extends to sharing a bathroom with strangers, *ma chère madame,* perhaps I've misjudged you, and you're not as bright as I took you to be."

He made it sound as if she planned to indulge in a group back-scrubbing session with her fellow guests, but she knew when she was being baited, and refused to be drawn in. "Perhaps you have," she said. "And just for the record, I'm not your *chère* anything. Now run off and torment someone else."

"All in good time," he replied, unfazed by her rejection and instead flashing her a smile that made her heart turn over. She'd thought him handsome enough last night, but now, in the sun-splashed light of morning, the full extent of his male beauty became apparent. "First, tell me what you have planned for today."

Involuntarily her gaze swung to Henri, busy wiping down the other outdoor tables. "Nothing special."

Following her gaze, he drawled with unmistakable innuendo, "Indeed? If I didn't know better, I'd say, from the hungry glance you just cast at your host, that you have something very specific in mind."

For heaven's sake, the man could very well turn out to be her uncle! "Are you implying I plan to seduce a man old enough to be my father?" she asked, unable to stifle a burst of incredulous laughter.

"Not at all. I don't think he's quite your type, and even if he was, his wife would take a cast iron skillet to your skull before you so much as laid a hand on him. But there are other ways of taking advantage of someone, particularly if a person has a hidden agenda." He leaned closer, a sudden coating of steel overlaying his deep velvet voice. "But that couldn't possibly be the case with you, could it, Diana? You wouldn't try to exploit a man as harmless as Henri for your personal gain, would you?"

He knows what you're up to, her inner voice whispered, even as her common sense questioned how that could possibly be so. She'd confided only in Carol, and Carol would never betray her secret.

Bolstered by the realization, she said with a commendable

veneer of scorn, "Dear me, are you this protective of everyone in the village, or just a select few?"

"Every last one, Diana," he declared flatly. "These people have stood shoulder to shoulder with my family for centuries, and in more recent times, proved their loyalty to me in ways I'll never forget. So you may be assured I'll come down with a very heavy hand on anyone looking to take advantage of them."

"I'll bear that in mind," she said. "Now, if that's all…?"

He stood up, all lithe, elegant six feet plus of him blocking out the sun and leaving her chilled in his shade. "That's all—unless you decide to take me up on my proposition, that is, in which case, by all means feel free to get in touch." He dropped a business card on the table. "You can reach me at this number, anytime."

Hell will freeze over first, Monsieur le Comte! she thought, watching as he stalked away. *I'll go home empty-handed before I turn to you for anything.*

She was still simmering with resentment when Henri emerged from the kitchen, carrying a basket of hot rolls, a flat dish of butter curls and a little pot of preserves. "For your *petit déjeuner,*" he announced, setting them before her, and spreading a red linen napkin over her lap. "Would you like more coffee to go with them?"

The little square was deserted, and the inn only just stirring to life. Not about to squander such a heaven-sent opportunity, she said, "Thank you, I would, Henri, and I'd like it even better if you poured a cup for yourself and kept me company a while."

He agreed willingly enough, settling his bulk on the hard metal chair, a thick cup of black coffee cradled between his big hands. "My wife made the *confitures* from berries my granddaughter picked last week," he told her, watching as she buttered a roll, "and the brioches I baked myself, just this morning."

"You take care of all the meals, do you?"

"*Oui, madame!* Cooking is what I do best."

"Don't you get tired, working such long hours?"

"I'm used to it," he said, cheerfully. "It is my life, and I have five brothers I can count on for extra help, should I need it."

She could have pretended this was the first she'd heard about his large family, but she was already knee-deep enough in lies she'd have preferred to avoid and saw no point in compounding them unnecessarily. "So Monsieur de Valois told me, last night." She paused, filled with trepidation, now that the moment she'd anticipated was finally at hand. In the next few minutes, he could breathe new life into her hopes, or dash them to pieces.

Her heart thudded so violently, she was sure Henri must be able to hear it; could surely see how its fluttering agitation made the front of her blouse quiver. "Five brothers…but also a sister as well, right?"

His face lit up. *"Mais certainement, madame!* My sister, Jeanne."

"Does she help you out here, too?"

"She would, if she had the time," he said. "But she is kept too busy running the château for le Comte."

"She works for the…him?"

Her question exploded in shock before she could contain it, but Henri didn't appear to notice anything amiss. *"Oui.* She is his…" He tugged at his earlobe, searching without success to find the right word. "In French, we call her his *gouvernante."*

"His housekeeper?"

"Exactly so, *madame.* She and her husband have been employed at the château for many years. Since they were newlyweds, some twenty-five years ago, in fact. Gregoire is in charge of the vineyards, and—"

"She got married when she was nineteen?"

Too late, she realized her slip. "How did you know that, *madame?"* Henri inquired, narrow-eyed suddenly.

Floundering, she stammered, "Well, I didn't, not really. It was a wild guess, based on the fact that Monsieur de Valois said she was fifteen years…younger than…you…."

"And why would he tell you my age?"

She closed her eyes, and wished she'd done the same with her mouth, before she managed to put both feet in it.

You'll never carry this off, Carol had predicted. *You're just not the undercover type. Sooner or later, you'll trip yourself up—and knowing you, it'll probably be sooner.*

How right she'd been!

"Because I said you seem much too young to be a grandfather," she babbled, desperately trying to patch the holes she'd inadvertently poked in the fabric of her cover-up. "You know how we Americans are, Henri—obsessed with our weight and age, to the exclusion of just about everything else. For a man of your years to look so youthful…well, you'd be the envy of people half your age, in my country."

She was stretching the truth considerably, but she'd learned well, during her marriage, the need to stroke a man's ego when necessary, and could only hope Henri was as susceptible to flattery as her ex-husband had been.

It appeared that he was. "It is the diet," he proclaimed mollified. "The olive oil is good for the skin, the garlic good for the health and the tomatoes good for the manliness."

She wasn't sure quite what he meant by his last remark, nor did she care to find out. His masculine prowess was none of her business. His sister, however, very well might be. "Something must be working in the women's favor, too," she suggested lightly. "Imagine having seven children, and six of them boys! Your mother deserves a medal. Were you all born here?"

"*Oui, madame.* All seven of us in the same house, on Rue Sainte Agathe, where my youngest brother now stays with his wife and three children, and to this day we all live within a few miles of each other. It is the way to keep families close."

Diana couldn't have asked for a better lead-in. "I suppose it is, but did none of you ever want to go farther afield, and see a bit more of the world?"

"Never the boys," he said, little realizing what a loaded question she'd asked. "We were working men from the day we finished our schooling."

"What about your sister?"

He grimaced. "Ah, Jeanne was different—a rebel, if you like, with her head full of unrealistic dreams."

Sensing she was on the brink of vital discovery, Diana struggled to keep a lid on her excitement. "Unrealistic how?"

"She wanted too much, more than she had a right to expect, and when she decided she wouldn't find it here, she ran away from home when she was only sixteen, leaving behind nothing but a note saying she had gone to Marseille. The shame almost killed our mother and father."

"Shame?"

"*Oui, madame.* Society sees things differently now, but in those days, good girls did not risk their reputations by acting so recklessly. My little sister darkened our family name with her actions."

Good girls? Diana almost choked on her anger. How about *frightened* girls? *Desperate* girls? Girls who made a mistake and had no one to turn to in their trouble? Or didn't they count? Was it only the sons who mattered? "Didn't you at least try to find her?"

"*Bien sûr!* My brothers and I searched the streets of Marseille for many days. But it is a large city, and unless you have tried to locate someone who doesn't wish to be found, you cannot know how impossible a task you set yourself."

Not impossible, Henri, Diana thought, her heart bleeding for the young woman who increasingly fit the mold of her lost mother. *You just have to want it badly enough not to be fooled by false leads.* "So what are you saying? That you gave up on her?"

"Never that! But we were not miracle workers, and by then had wives and babies of our own waiting for us here, at home. Jeanne had chosen to follow a wild path, and in the end, she had to live with that."

Containing herself with difficulty, Diana said, "How would you ever have forgiven yourselves, if something bad had happened to her?"

"Ah, but we knew she was alive and well, because every once in a while, she would phone here, to the inn, and tell us so."

At that, Diana's rage spilled over. For grown men to be so willfully naive struck her as unforgivable. *"And you believed her?"*

"What other choice did we have?" Henri raised his hands, palms up, and rolled his eyes. "We learned to be content with what she gave us, and to hear her voice was better than silence. She had made her choice, and there was nothing we could do but accept it, and hope she would eventually come back to us. Which, after several months, she did." A beatific smile split his face. "What is it they say, that there's no place like home?"

"How did she explain her absence?"

"She didn't," he admitted. "She never spoke a word of how she made enough money to live on."

"And it never occurred to you to ask?"

He flung her a dark glance. "A pretty girl, with no means of supporting herself, alone in a city like Marseille? We were better off not knowing! It was enough that she'd learned her lesson. As she most surely had. Even though my parents forgave her and welcomed her with open arms, she wasn't the same girl who'd left us, almost seven months earlier. There was a pensiveness to her, an air of that sorrow that clung to her like a mist which never disperses, no matter how hot the sun might shine. She has it still, to this day."

You'd have it, too, if your firstborn was taken from your arms and given to strangers! "Poor girl. She was so young—too young, to bear so much alone."

"She was not alone for very long," Henri said, misunderstanding. "Within a very short time, she fell in love with Gregoire Delancie. They became engaged a year later, and married a year after that. She was fortunate that such a good man wanted her. To many, she would have been considered soiled goods. As it was, she had a husband, and the Mesdames de Valois, who were by then living at the château, were so kind as to offer her respectable work."

Doing what? Catering to the boy who was to become Count? Cooking his meals, laundering his clothes, picking up after him and generally being at his beck and call, twenty-four hours a day? Again, Diana had to swallow her indignation.

"She is a very lucky woman," Henri stated, heaving himself to his feet. "And I will be one very sorry man if my wife discovers me gossiping with you, when I should be preparing the ratatouille for tonight's meal." He gave her a quaint little bow. "*À toute à l'heure, madame!* It was a pleasure talking to you."

"Yes," Diana replied with a smile, though her next move already taking shape in her mind. "See you later, Henri."

Anton's card remained where he'd dropped it on the table.

Half an hour earlier, she'd have said nothing would induce her to touch it. Now, though, she reached for it gingerly, wishing there was some other way, one that wouldn't involve such a complete loss of face. But pride had no place in her dilemma. As the old saying went, she couldn't afford to look a gift horse in the mouth, not even one as disturbingly attractive as the incomparable Count, not when he presented the means for her to get to know the woman she was now convinced was her birth mother.

He picked up his phone on the first ring.

"I've given the matter some thought and changed my mind," she informed him, plunging into what she had to say without preamble, before she gagged on the humiliation of having to retract her previously scornful dismissal of his proposition. "If your offer from this morning still stands, I'm prepared to accept it."

So help her, she thought, holding her breath, if he gloated, she'd slam down the phone so hard, he'd rupture an eardrum.

But, "The offer still stands, Diana," he said neutrally. "How soon can you start?"

"How soon would you like me to start?"

"This afternoon. Get your stuff together, and I'll pick you up."

"There's no need for that. I have my own car."

"If it's that pitiful piece of junk parked behind the inn, it's leaking oil and has a flat tire."

"Then I'll rent something else."

"I'm afraid not. The nearest leasing outfit is fifty kilometers east of here, so stop arguing and start packing. I'll be there in half an hour."

Who did he think he was talking to? Grinding her teeth in fury, she fought the impulse to tell him to take his job and stuff it down his throat, and instead replied meekly, "That doesn't give me much time, Anton."

"Half an hour, Diana," he repeated implacably, and broke the connection.

He drove a dark green Range Rover that smelled of leather and money. "Are you going to tell me what brought about such a sudden change of heart?" he asked, sparing her a fleeting glance before returning his attention to the road winding through shady olive groves and neat vineyards, to the château on the hill.

"I decided the positives of helping you outweighed the negatives," she said blandly, having prepared herself to answer just such a question. "I enjoy meeting people, and I've never lived in a castle before."

His mouth curved in amusement. "Come now, Diana! It was having to share a bathroom at the inn that persuaded you."

"That, too," she said, reminding herself she couldn't afford to like this man too much. But that did nothing to diminish the impact of his smile.

Harvey seldom smiled at all, unless he was trying to impress someone, she recalled, and even then, his mouth remained pinched, as if the effort pained him. "Medicine is serious business," he used to say. "The things I see on the operating table don't leave much room for levity."

Why did it take Anton de Valois for her to recognize such a statement for the pretentious nonsense it was?

"I asked my housekeeper to prepare a suite for you," Anton continued, steering around the last bend in the road. "Although the original château was built over six hundred years ago, much has been done to bring it into the twenty-first century, and I think you'll find it very comfortable. Once you're settled in, we'll have lunch, and talk about what your work entails."

Up close, the château and its surroundings were even more breathtaking than from a distance. Immediately ahead, a long, straight avenue bordered by Lombardy poplars ended at what was once a fortified gateway.

The house itself sat on a small rise, with sweeping views of the vineyards and more distant lavender fields. Dark blue slate covered the steep mansard roof, but the walls were of stone, dappled in shades varying from palest lemon to deep honey-gold by the angle of the sun. Flowers bracketed the doorways and spilled exuberantly from windowsills rising three stories from the ground. Above them, graceful turrets and parapets gleamed against a background of intense blue sky.

Diana stared, awestruck. The closest she'd ever come to such a spectacular scene was in the books of fairy tales she'd devoured as a child. "Anton, your home is magnificent!"

"It has its drawbacks," he said, "but for the most part, it'll do."

"You must need an army of staff to look after it."

"A small army to tend the grounds and take care of general maintenance, certainly, but not that many to look after the running of the house. Except for special occasions, when I bring in outside help, we get by with a housekeeper, cook and four maids."

"That seems like a lot, for just three people."

"I like to spread the load. It might have been acceptable in the old days for household staff to work fourteen-hour days, seven days a week, but it's not my idea of fair treatment."

Well, she could hardly take issue with that sentiment. "I'm sure your employees appreciate your consideration."

Another smile touched his mouth. "It cuts both ways, Diana. Treat people well, and they generally give back in kind."

They'd reached the top of the avenue by then. The Range Rover cruised under the gateway and into a forecourt where another vehicle, an old Mercedes convertible covered in dust, was parked haphazardly to one side of the steps leading to the château's massive front door.

At the sight of it, Anton's expression darkened forbiddingly. "I hope that doesn't mean what I think it does," he growled.

As if she'd been waiting for her cue to appear, a woman stepped out from the château's dim interior. "Surprise, Anton!" she trilled in a throaty contralto, slinking down the steps with the stealthy grace of some exotic, overbred cat.

Heaving a sigh, he stepped out of the car, submitted to her embrace and replied with markedly less enthusiasm, "Hello, Sophie. Surprise, indeed. I wasn't expecting you."

Not the least put out by his cool reception, she laughed and, with the kind of confidence Diana envied, cooed, "But now that I'm here, you're glad to see me, *oui?*"

"As long as you don't mind keeping yourself entertained. I can't spare much time to play host."

"With you, *mon cher,*" she replied, winding her arm through his and leaning against him suggestively, "a little goes a very long way!"

Feeling very much like a third wheel, Diana slid out of the Range Rover and tried to blend into the background, but she'd have done better to remain out of sight in the car. Belatedly realizing that he'd not arrived alone, Sophie unglued herself from Anton's side, and fixed Diana in a stare that stripped her to the bone. "And who, may I ask, is this?"

"Diana Reeves," he said, starting to unload Diana's luggage from the back of the Range Rover.

"And she's moving in with you?" Sophie's formerly purring tones soared dramatically.

"Oui. She has very kindly agreed to conduct tours of the château and gardens, until such time as I can find someone else to take on the job."

"Oh, just an *employee!"* Sophie flipped her elegant hand dismissively. "You had me worried, *mon cher* Anton! For a moment, I thought she was *someone."*

"Stop behaving badly, Sophie, or I'll send you packing," he warned her severely. "Diana, this is Sophie Beauvais, a distant cousin on my mother's side of the family, and I apologize for her appalling manners, since it's unlikely that she'll see fit to do so."

"Hi," Diana said, and left it at that, since it was obvious the woman wasn't the least bit interested in being introduced to anyone who wasn't *someone.*

But that one word was enough to send Sophie's eyebrows shooting skyward. "You're American?"

"Yes."

"Well, unless you have a permit, you're not allowed to work while you're here."

"Technically she's not working, because she's not accepting payment for services," Anton intervened. "She's simply a houseguest who's offered to help out a friend, and that, I believe, is perfectly legitimate, no matter where she's from."

"I'm not sure the authorities would agree, Anton."

She had to be the most unpleasant creature in the whole of France, and the thought of having to placate her, enough to turn a person's stomach. But it was either that, or risk having her entire plan of operation derailed, and Diana had come too far to allow that to happen. "Look at it this way," she said, gagging inwardly at the conciliatory tone she was forced to adopt. "My being here frees Anton to spend more time with you."

Sophie regarded her a moment, eyes narrowed appraisingly. "I hadn't thought of it in that light. Perhaps keeping you around isn't such a bad idea, after all."

"Of course it's not." Taking perverse pleasure in the killing glare Anton directed at her behind his cousin's back, Diana continued, "Just enjoy your visit, and forget I'm even here."

The truce, if indeed it could be called that, soon ended. "You're forgotten already, *mademoiselle*," the revolting creature declared, turning away. "Anton, *mon cher,* let one of the hired help lug those suitcases inside, and pour me a glass of wine before lunch, won't you?"

"I'll pour us all a glass. Come with me, Diana." He cupped her elbow, and under cover of ushering her up the steps, muttered grimly, "*Mon dieu,* you're turning out to be more trouble than you're worth!"

"I have no idea what you're talking about," she said, his warm breath arousing such unmentionable sensations in her ear that she went weak at the knees.

"Certainly you do, trying to land me in the hot seat with that woman! Obviously I'm going to have to set out a few ground rules, but it'll have to wait because, right now, my housekeeper is waiting to greet you."

She looked up then, and at the sight of the woman standing in the shadow of the great doorway, everything to do with him and his obnoxious cousin fled Diana's mind. Her breath froze, her palms grew damp, her throat closed and her senses swam to the point that she was afraid she might pass out.

"Diana," Anton said, his words seeming to float toward her from very far away, "may I introduce my housekeeper, Jeanne Delancie. Jeanne, this is Diana Reeves, our house guest."

"*Bonjour, madame,*" the housekeeper said, the singsong accent of Provence gentle in her voice. "*Bienvenue au Château de Valois.*"

Of course, it was her mother. Her eyes were not blue, as

she'd expected, but one glance into their clear brown depths, and that visceral instinct Diana had relied on to guide her, told her with utter certainty that she'd come face-to-face, at last, with her birth mother.

It was all she could do not to fling herself into the woman's arms and burst out crying. Fortunately Anton retained a firm enough grip on her elbow to make such a move impossible.

CHAPTER FIVE

"She's never going to be able to handle the job, Anton. For pity's sake, she could hardly bring herself to speak to that housekeeper of yours. How do you suppose she's going to cope with a mob of tourists plying her with questions?"

"I'm sure she'll be perfectly fine," he said, which was an outright lie. Although not about to admit it to Sophie, he'd been completely taken aback by Diana's tongue-tied response to Jeanne.

His cousin held out her glass for a refill. "That's easy to say, but how much do you really know about her?"

Not nearly enough, obviously. Just when he thought he had a handle on what she was all about, she challenged his perceptions yet again. How she could have dealt so skillfully with Sophie, who had to be the most volatile and contrary individual he ever hoped to meet, yet not be able to string two words together with soft-spoken, softhearted Jeanne, added one more layer to the enigma calling herself Diana Reeves. "Perhaps she's shy."

"She's socially inept, *mon amour!* Wherever did you find her?"

"She was staying at the inn. I ran into her by accident, last night."

Sophie let fly with a squawk of laughter. "Staying at the inn? That should have been enough to tell you she's not the sharpest knife in the drawer! No one, least of all an American used to the very latest in modern conveniences, would willingly subject herself to the primitive conditions *that* place has to offer."

In his view, the unpretentious simplicity of the inn was its most appealing characteristic, but Sophie's conclusions regarding American women's tastes in hotel accommodation coincided exactly with his own. Again not disposed to share the fact with Sophie, he shrugged and said idly, "Why else do you think I invited her to stay here?"

"Because you're much too gallant for your own good— although turning over the Ivory Suite to her wasn't very kind when you know it's my favorite place to stay when I'm visiting." She eyed him coyly over the rim of her glass. "On the other hand, the suite I've been assigned is much closer to yours."

God preserve me! he thought, making a mental note to lock his door every night. "Exactly why *did* you decide on this sudden visit, Sophie? The last I heard, you were playing house with some man in Paris."

"He bored me to tears. All he cared about was his work. We'd never have made a go of it together, so I moved out."

In other words, he wasn't prepared to be your next meal ticket and kicked you out! "I'm sorry."

"Don't be," she said, tucking one leg under her and managing to display several inches of sleek thigh in the process. "I'm not interested in another divorce. My next husband is going to be my last."

"After three failed marriages, I'm surprised you'd even consider a fourth."

"It'll be different, the next time. Before, I've made do with second best, because the man I really wanted wasn't available, but that's no longer the case." She dipped her finger in her wine. "Marie-Louise has been gone almost three years. Don't you miss having a wife, Anton? A sympathetic ear to listen to your troubles, after a hard day? A warm, willing body in your bed at night?"

He didn't care for the hungry gleam in her eye, or the suggestive way she slipped her finger in her mouth, then drew it slowly out again. He had nothing against marriage, or sex, but he'd gladly swear off both before he got involved in either with his cousin, Sophie. He wasn't fond of black widow spiders.

Just then, Diana came out to the terrace. "Hope I haven't kept you waiting," she said, appearing more herself again. "I decided to unpack my suitcases before I came down for lunch."

"Your timing's perfect," he assured her, more grateful for her interruption than she could begin to realize. "How do you like your rooms?"

"Oh, they're…luxurious! My goodness, I feel like a princess!"

And if it weren't for the fact that you're the most duplicitous woman I've ever met, you could well pass for one, he thought, taking note of her elegant carriage. "I'm glad you're pleased. If there's anything you need, you have only to ask Jeanne."

"I know. She told me the same thing." She ducked her head diffidently, once again adopting the role of a naif suddenly unsure of herself in sophisticated company. "She was very kind, very helpful."

"Why wouldn't she be, Diana?" he asked silkily. "Unless you're presenting yourself as something you're not, I'm sure she'll take great pleasure in making you feel right at home."

Her blush told him his comment had found its mark, and part of him took savage satisfaction in knowing he was one step ahead of her and whatever scheme she was cooking up. But another part—a weaker part he despised—experienced a stab of disappointment that she couldn't be as sweetly innocent as she so often seemed.

"That's more than can be said for the way your housekeeper treats me," Sophie pouted. "Frankly, Anton, I don't find her very welcoming at all."

Switching personalities yet again, Diana spoke up in spirited defense of the woman whom, at first sight, she'd appeared to find intimidating. "Perhaps because she has enough to do running such a large household, without the aggravation of having guests drop in unexpectedly."

"If you feel that strongly, perhaps *you* should lend her a hand—when you're not fulfilling your other duties around here, that is," Sophie retaliated.

In no mood to referee a catfight, Anton seated Diana on his left, put Sophie on his right and heaved an audible sigh of relief as the maids showed up to serve lunch.

The best part of the meal, Diana decided, was not the cold cucumber soup, or prawns in aspic, wonderful though they were, but the fact that the inimical Sophie pretty much drank herself into a stupor and staggered off to take a siesta before dessert and coffee were served.

"I don't think she approves of me," she told Anton ruefully, still smarting from some of his cousin's more barbed remarks.

"Don't take it personally," he said. "Sophie doesn't like too many women, especially not those she perceives to be a threat."

A startled laugh escaped her. "Oh, please! I can hardly be considered a threat!"

His mouth tightened ominously. "False modesty ill becomes you, Diana. You've looked in the mirror. You know very well that most men find you attractive. Even Henri has fallen under your spell."

But not you, she thought, wondering what had brought about his black mood. He'd been unusually curt throughout lunch, and at first she'd put it down to his irritation with Sophie's constant need to be the center of attention. Now, though, with his cousin removed from the scene, he seemed more annoyed than ever.

"Are you upset with me, Anton?" she ventured. "Have I done something to offend you?"

He flung her a glance simmering with pent-up emotion.

Passion…or anger? She couldn't tell. Knew only that the air between them crackled with tension.

"If I didn't know better," he said, wrestling himself under control, "I'd say you had a guilty conscience. Of course, I'd be mistaken…wouldn't I?"

"Not entirely," she admitted, running her tongue over lips suddenly gone dry. "I feel I'm imposing on your hospitality. All this…" She indicated the china and heavy sterling cutlery, both embossed with the de Valois family crest, the cut crystal water goblets. "Well, it's rather more opulent than what I expected when I agreed to work for you. I'd feel a lot more comfortable if we could get down to business and you told me exactly what my duties entail. If I'm going to take on the job, I'd like to do it well."

"It's really quite simple. If you're done with your meal—"

"I'm done."

He rose abruptly from the table. "Then rather than tell you what's involved, I'll show you. Come with me."

She followed him to the grand entrance hall. "Since the tour groups assemble here, we'll start on this level, and work our way up," he began. "Notice that the floors and stairs are made of carrara marble, imported from Italy. The château itself is over six hundred years old and has seen a number of changes over the centuries, not all of them desirable, but my grandfather embarked on a complete restoration to preserve the integrity of the original design, while implementing modern innovations that make it not just a historical treasure, but a comfortable home for me and my heirs."

"That's a lot of information to digest, and you've barely begun," she said, desperate to ease the tension still arcing between them. "Should I be making notes on the palm of my hand?"

"No." He fixed her in an unsmiling glance. "You should stop interrupting and pay attention."

"I'm trying to, but—"

"Try harder," he snapped, and manacling her wrist in an iron grip, drew her behind him as he marched across the hall. "Certain areas only are open to the public. The family's apartments are private, as you'd expect. Here on the main floor, we have the chapel, the ballroom, the formal banquet hall and the entrance to the wine cellar. One floor up, you'll find the library, the formal drawing room and the ladies' parlor. And among other things on the top floor, the bedroom where a seventeenth-century Pope, Clement the Eighth, is reputed to have slept."

She nodded as if she was obediently drinking in everything he told her when, if truth be known, she was so vividly conscious of his fingers wrapped around her wrist, so powerfully entrapped in his magnetic field, that he might as well have been speaking in ancient tongues.

At such close quarters, she could detect his aftershave and just the faintest shadow of new beard darkening his lean jaw. Every time he glanced at her, his lashes swept down, dense and black above the dramatic silver-gray of his irises. His dark hair lay thick and glossy against his well-shaped head.

Unaware that her mind was straying, he continued to pepper her with information. "The family quarters are roped off, although you'll have to keep an eye out for the odd tourist who tries to sneak away from the group and go poking around in places he doesn't belong, but once you're familiar with the layout of the place, you won't have any trouble."

I'm already knee-deep in trouble, she thought, wishing he was revoltingly obese, or effeminate, or had chronically bad breath, instead of being so thoroughly masculine and utterly, perfectly beautiful that all she could do was fixate on his mouth and wonder how it would taste against hers. How it would feel, sliding over the heated skin of her body. "And the grounds?" she inquired faintly.

Still oblivious to his detrimental effect on her faculties, he steered her up the stairs to a large leaded window on the first landing, which overlooked a sweeping view of the south side

gardens. "Again, fairly straightforward," he practically barked.
"You conduct a walking tour of the area immediately below the
balustraded terrace down there, pointing out the ornamental
fountain, the parterre, the orange grove and the hundred-year-
old oak trees on the island in the middle of the man-made lake.
If you like, you may stop by the crypt—you can see its roof
just beyond that stand of pines to your right—where genera-
tions of de Valoises lay entombed, but not everyone's into burial
sites, so you have to use your judgment on that one."

But I don't trust my judgment anymore, she thought helplessly. *If I did, I wouldn't be allowing my thoughts to stray to
matters totally inappropriate both to the present situation, and
my personal circumstances. I've just come out of a marriage I
thought would last forever. To be entertaining sexual fantasies
about any man, least of all this proud, autocratic Frenchman,
is emotional suicide.*

"This area usually arouses a lot of interest, so you might
need to brush up on your art history," he went on, turning down
a long gallery on the third floor, whose walls were lined with
paintings. "For example, this is a Renoir, and there's a Cara-
vaggio over there, with a Rubens hanging next to it."

"Don't you worry someone might try to steal them?"

"Not in the least. They're wired to an alarm system. Anyone
so much as touches a frame, and all hell breaks loose at the
central switchboard."

The gallery was fairly dim, probably because the only
lighting came from concealed floods designed to showcase the
art, but one painting, a portrait of a couple, done in oils, drew
her attention. "I don't recognize this artist or the subject. Is it
very well-known?"

"No," Anton said. "It's of my great-grandparents, and was
painted by a friend of theirs, in the late 1930s."

Unlike most stiffly-posed, husband-wife portraits of that
era, this couple had been depicted in the château gardens. She

half-reclined at his feet, all dreamy elegance in a flowing, blush-pink dress, with a Japanese parasol at her side. He smiled down at her from his high-backed wicker chair, his hand resting on her shoulder. "They look as if they were very much in love."

"I'm told they were," he said briefly, turning away.

But Diana lingered, cast them one last glance, then, to her horror, heard herself ask, "Did you love your wife?"

He stopped dead in his tracks, his spine so rigid, he might have been turned to stone. "Of course I did."

She should let the matter drop there. Be satisfied that he hadn't told her in no uncertain terms that his relationship with his late wife was none of her business. But she couldn't help herself. She had to know more. "Do you still mourn her death?"

"Not the way I once did. Why is this of interest to you?"

"I'm wondering how long it takes to get over losing someone."

"I'd say that depends on the individual, and the reason the connection was broken."

"I thought I'd never stop loving Harvey, but now I find myself wondering what it was I ever saw in him. Is it wrong, do you think, that I'm already forgetting what he looks like?"

"Not wrong at all. It's a sign that you're ready to put the past to rest, and move on."

Ironically they'd reached the end of the gallery and could go no farther because a heavy door blocked access to the remainder of that part of the house. Although he no longer held her by the wrist, Anton stood close enough for his body to brush hers as he swung back to face her. She had to crane her neck to look at him. To look into those remarkable eyes, which could change in an instant from dusky moonlight to stormy gray. And at that moment, the storm reigned supreme, filling them with anguish.

"Move on to what?" she asked.

Their glances held. His breath caught. He lifted his hand. Let it ghost over her hair and down her cheek. "This," he ground out, and brought his mouth down on hers.

She thought it would end there; that he'd quickly pull away and swipe the back of his hand over his mouth to rid himself of the taste of her. Instead he lifted his head just long enough to cradle her face between his palms, then kissed her again.

She'd been kissed before, and not only by Harvey, but never in quite the way that Anton de Valois went about it. His mouth was an instrument of sublime torture beside which all other men's faded into insignificance, not because he used his tongue or teeth to seduce her, but because he teamed raging passion with circumspection, and turned them into an art that left her aching. Rather than tightening in rejection, her lips softened beneath his in total submission. Instead of shoving him away, as any woman with a grain of concern for self-preservation would have, she sank against him and clutched a fistful of his shirt.

It wasn't right. She wasn't ready for such an experience. But telling herself so didn't prevent the taut suspense in her body from finding release in a sudden damp explosion between her thighs. Most humiliating of all, it didn't silence the pitiful little moan that escaped her throat when he at last ended the kiss and she sagged, weak-kneed, against the door at her back. *Dear heaven!*

"I shouldn't have done that," he muttered harshly, his chest heaving and torment etched in every line of his face, "but I'd be lying if I didn't say I'd like to do it again."

"Why don't you, then?" she whispered.

Disgust darkened his expression. "Because we're both past the age to be making out in dark corners like a couple of hormone-driven teenagers."

Quickly, before she passed beyond all shame and begged him to take her somewhere more private where they could behave like consenting adults, she said shakily, "Yes, we certainly are. So to get back to business, what else is there to see up here?"

He held her gaze for a moment before replying. "The bedchamber where the Pope supposedly slept. It's the first room on the left as you come into the gallery. During the tours, the door is left open, with a small viewing area just inside. Of the remaining two suites, one is a baby's nursery, furnished as it would have been in the seventeenth century, with nanny quarters attached, and the other a governess's apartment, complete with small classroom. We'll take a look at them before we leave."

"And this door, here?" Unlike the rest, which were heavily carved, with wide, ornate casings, the one blocking off the end of the gallery consisted of a solid oak slab of more recent vintage, although the keyhole was large and elaborate to complement the antiquity of those on the remaining doors.

"Leads to the east wing and is kept locked at all times."

"Why?"

"Because that part of the château is no longer in use."

That she'd said the wrong thing again was immediately apparent. His tone was glacial, his expression remote, his eyes the color of flint. "I'm sorry I asked," she said.

"Forget it. You had no way of knowing."

Forget it? How was that possible, when, after a cursory glance into the aforementioned rooms, he swept her through the rest of the château, so clearly anxious to complete the tour and be rid of her that she could barely keep up with him?

"…coffered ceiling in the library…rare first editions…family bible on table…recorded births and deaths going back four hundred years…seating for a hundred in the banquet hall…still used on occasion…same with ballroom…frescoed dome there merits extra attention…floor highly polished…make sure no one steps off the runners…don't need any lawsuits…."

He rattled off facts, spitting them out like bullets as he fairly raced her through the remaining rooms. Then, returning to the great hall just as the long case clock struck three, he informed her that he had other matters requiring his attention, that cocktails were at seven, that they dressed for dinner at eight, but not black tie except on special occasions, that she'd do well to review what she'd learned, and prepare herself to start conducting visitors on Tuesday of the following week.

"That allows you plenty of time to settle in, find your way around and learn what you need to know," he finished.

"You've got to be kidding!" she exclaimed, but might as well have saved her breath because, lord of the manor to the core, he'd already stalked away down the hall to what she presumed must be the west wing, leaving her, lowly hand-maiden that she was, standing there dumbfounded and wondering what the devil she'd gotten herself into.

"It's a lot to take in all at once, isn't it?" another, kinder voice observed, and looking up, Diana found Jeanne observing her from the same corridor down which Anton had disappeared.

"A lot?" She blew out a frustrated breath. "It's impossible!" *He* was impossible!

"Try not to worry. It'll all fall into place, you'll see."

"I'm not so sure of that." She pressed her fingers to her throbbing temples. "Everything's so jumbled up in my head, it feels as if it's about to burst."

Her mother touched her arm sympathetically. "Let me make you a cup of tea, *madame*. It'll help you relax."

A rush of tears barely held in check caught Diana by surprise. I'm not Madame, I'm your daughter! she ached to say, but knew she couldn't, not yet, and perhaps never. Perhaps she'd eventually leave this place with her mother none the wiser of the bond they shared.

"Madame? You would like tea?"

"Thank you, I'd love some, but only if you'll join me." Then, sensing her mother's hesitation, she rushed to add, "Please, Jeanne! You'd be doing me an enormous favor. As I understand it, you've worked here for so long, you must know the place like the back of your hand, and I desperately need some help sorting out my information."

"Well, if you don't mind coming to my office…?"

"I don't mind."

In truth, she'd have walked over fire for the chance to spend more time alone with her mother. The few minutes they'd shared when Jeanne had shown her to her suite of rooms had been all too brief.

Under any other circumstances, Diana would have been totally entranced by the restful ivory and sage-green decor of her little sitting room, with its silk upholstered love seat and lady's *escritoire;* by the four-poster bed in the large sleeping chamber, and the elegant appointments of the marble bathroom. But her attention had been focused mainly on Anton's housekeeper. She'd found no evidence, in Jeanne's steady gaze and gentle smile, of the young rebel who'd run away to bear a child alone. Rather, under that calm and kindly demeanor, she'd detected a woman tamed by grief. A woman designed all through to be a mother, but robbed of the opportunity.

Accompanying her now down the corridor to her office, Diana wasn't sure what to expect. Something low-ceilinged, cramped and distinctly "below stairs," probably. But the light, airy room into which she stepped was spacious, functional and charming.

Two large computer desks filled one wall, each with a window at eye level offering views of the stables and a hillside filled with ruler-straight rows of grapevines. Bookcases and filing cabinets took up space on another wall. A table filled the middle of the floor, piled with neat stacks of mail and brochures.

Next to where she stood, just inside the door, a calendar, the week's menus and a list of household supplies needing to be purchased were pinned to a cork board. On the fourth wall were mullioned doors, similar to those in her own suite, but where hers gave access to a narrow balcony, these opened to a walled courtyard large enough to accommodate a wrought-iron table shaded by an umbrella, two comfortable chairs, a ceramic planter overflowing with scarlet geraniums and a small stone fountain.

This was no corner of a damp, miserable basement, Diana had to admit, and nor was Jeanne its Cinderella. Her pale gray shirtdress was smart and fashionable, her shoes, though built for comfort, stylish. She wore lipstick, a trace of eye shadow, a hint of perfume. Pearl stud earrings peeked out beneath her short, curly hair, and an old-fashioned diamond engagement ring nested beside her wedding band.

"I'd like tea for two, please, Odette," she instructed, speaking into an intercom on the desk. "And a plate of shortbread, please."

At first, they sat in the courtyard, sipped fragrant Earl Grey tea and sampled little coins of lavender-studded shortbread so light they melted on the tongue. Then her mother pushed aside the tray and produced a floor plan of the château, the kind sold to tourists from the gift shop at the lavender distillery. With her help, Diana marked the route she'd follow when she conducted her tours and made notes of the facts she needed to memorize.

"You see?" Jeanne said, when they were done. "It's really not so complicated, after all. Basically the west wing is off-limits to the public. The family has exclusive use of the upper two floors. The Count's office, the administration office, central switchboard and staff quarters occupy the ground floor."

Diana knew she shouldn't, but she couldn't help herself. Still smarting from the way Anton had kissed her as if he couldn't get enough of her one minute, and shut her out completely, the next, she said, "Why is the upper east wing closed off?"

Her mother hesitated briefly, then lifted her shoulders in a faint, regretful shrug. "Maintaining a house as large as this is labor intensive and cost prohibitive. It makes no sense to waste time and money on rooms that stand empty all year and are of little historical interest to tourists."

"Has it never been used?"

"It was, once." Again, Jeanne hesitated. "But...not recently."

She seemed uncomfortable talking about it which, added to the way Anton had shut down on her when she'd questioned him on the same subject, served only to sharpen Diana's curiosity. But she could hardly remark on that to her mother, whose loyalty to her employer was evident.

Instead she turned the conversation to something that mattered to her a great deal more than a moldy set of empty rooms. "Do you enjoy your work here, Jeanne?"

"Very much. My husband and I are given free rein in our separate endeavors, treated with kindness and respect, and rewarded well for our labors. What more could we ask for?"

What, indeed? Yet for all that she seemed in cheerful command of her world, Henri had put it well when he said there was a stillness to Jeanne, a hint of sorrow that never went away. It showed in the sometimes faraway look in her big brown eyes, as if, no matter how pleasing the present might be, or how rosy the future, she couldn't quite let go of the past.

Or was that wishful thinking on her part, Diana wondered.

"So this is where you are, *mon ange,* whiling away the afternoon in idle gossip when you should be preparing my dinner!" The man stepping out of the château to lean over Jeanne's chair and drop a kiss on her head was tall and slender, with the nut-brown skin of one who'd spent a lifetime working long hours in the sun.

"Gregoire!" Jeanne sprang up from her seat, the lilt in her voice, the smile on her face, that of a young girl in love. "I didn't expect you back so soon. Madame Reeves, this is my dear husband, Gregoire."

"I am delighted to meet you, *madame,*" he said. "And I apologize if I was overly familiar with my remarks just now. I didn't realize you're a guest of the Count."

"I'm very happy to meet you, too," Diana said. "And I'm actually a working guest, which isn't quite the same thing. So will you both please forget the Madame Reeves business, and call me Diana?"

Gregoire Delancie's inscrutable blue eyes subjected her to

a thorough inspection. "If you wish. Jeanne, my love, you're needed in the kitchen. Something to do with the pear sauce for tonight's dessert, I'm told."

"Then I'd better see what's it's about." She turned to Diana with a smile. "You will excuse me, Diana?"

"Of course. I should be leaving anyway. Thank you, Jeanne. You've been a great help. Goodbye, Gregoire."

"Goodbye," he returned, stiffly enough that she knew without his having to say so that he hoped she wouldn't make a habit of invading their quarters. Nor, she noticed, did he use her given name.

Why doesn't he like me? she wondered, making her way back to the main part of the house and up the marble staircase.

Then she forgot about him completely because, as she reached the third-floor landing and turned into the west wing, she ran smack into Anton. And one look at his face was enough to tell her his mood was no sweeter now than it had been two hours ago.

Oh, for heaven's sake! What had she done, or not done, to find herself the object of *his* displeasure, as well? Why couldn't he turn back into that charming man from last night who seemed so thoroughly in charge of his world? Better yet, why couldn't he just take her in his arms, tell her how glad he was they'd met and kiss her again?

She found out soon enough.

CHAPTER SIX

"Where the devil have you been?" he demanded, taking refuge in anger, because pride wouldn't let him admit he'd been frantic at her disappearance. "I've spent the last hour and a half looking everywhere for you."

"Well, now you've found me," she said, wincing, "so please let go of my arm. You're hurting me."

He released her, shocked as much by the surge of relief that had swept over him at the sight of her, as he was by the red imprint of his fingers on her skin. "I was beginning to wonder if you'd run out on me."

"Don't think the idea didn't cross my mind."

"If I was abrupt with you earlier—"

"*Abrupt?* You were downright unpleasant!"

"It won't happen again."

"It had better not! If this afternoon was an example of what I've got to look forward to in the days ahead, you can find someone else to lead your benighted tour groups. You acted as if you'd caught me stealing the family silver, when all I did was ask a perfectly harmless question."

Harmless, Diana? he wondered, torn by conflicting emotions. *Maybe...or then again, maybe not.* "If that's the impression I gave, then I apologize. I didn't mean to offend you. The truth is, I was annoyed with myself, not you. I had no business kissing you."

"Oh." A flush tinted her face. "If it's all the same to you, I'd rather not talk about that. Can't we just forget it ever happened?"

You might be able to, he thought, the taste and feel of her so vivid in his mind that it was all he could do to keep his hands to himself, *but it'll be a long time before I can.*

In fact, it had been a long time since any woman had moved him so deeply, and *that,* if he was honest with himself, was the real root of the problem. He'd recovered from his wife's death—at least, as much as any man could, given the circumstances—and was ready to explore another relationship, but not with this enigmatic foreigner who played by rules different from the women he knew.

He'd lured her under his roof with one aim only: to uncover the real reason she'd chosen Bellevue-sur-Lac as her "holiday" destination. The phone call he'd overheard, her sudden about-face in accepting his job offer, and most especially, her frequent uneasiness around him, all pointed to an ulterior motive. Even now, with no logical reason to be nervous, she was worrying the sheet of paper she held, repeatedly rolling and unrolling it.

He'd be a fool to complicate matters further by allowing sex to enter the equation. No man was at his sharpest when he was between the sheets with a woman as beautiful as Diana Reeves.

"Well?" She tapped her dainty foot impatiently.

"Certainly we can forget it," he said. "We'll wipe the slate clean and start afresh, as of now."

"Thank you." Clearly braced for yet another confrontation, she continued to eye him warily. "So, why were you looking for me?"

"My aunts arrived home from their weekly jaunt to Aix and were anxious to meet you."

Her expression underwent a change. Grew open and filled with unfeigned warmth and interest. "So much has happened today, I'd forgotten they live with you. I'd love to meet them."

"Well, I'm afraid you'll have to postpone the pleasure until you join us for cocktails. They're dressing for dinner, now."

"Good heavens, is it that time, already? Then I should be getting dressed, too."

"Not until you answer my question," he said.

"What question is that?"

"Where did you go this afternoon, after I left you?"

"Nowhere. I was here the entire time."

"Then how is it that I couldn't find you?"

She shrugged insolently. "What can I say? You must have been looking in the wrong place. Now, if you don't mind…?"

She went to slip past him, but anticipating her move, he threw out his arm and blocked her escape. "I mind," he said flatly.

"That's your problem, Anton."

She tried to elbow him aside, and in doing so, dropped the rolled-up sheet of paper. It fluttered to the floor and landed at his feet. Smothering an exclamation of annoyance, she bent to retrieve it, but he was quicker, scooping it up before she could lay hands on it.

Recognizing it at once as part of a tourist information brochure showing the floor plan of the château, he said, "You were at the gift shop?"

"No."

"Then where did you get this?"

Another, deeper flush stained her cheeks. "Well, I didn't steal it, if that's what you're thinking."

"Don't be ridiculous! I'm thinking no such thing."

"If you must know, Jeanne gave it to me."

Puzzled, he said, "My housekeeper? Why didn't you say so in the first place?"

"I didn't want to land her in trouble. She was only trying to help me get a better fix on the layout of the château."

"Why would she be in trouble for that?"

"Because we had tea together. In her office." She flung the confession at him defiantly.

"So? Jeanne's free to entertain whomever she pleases—in her office, and just about anywhere else in this house, for that matter. She's practically a member of the family."

"Tell that to her husband. When he showed up, he couldn't get me out of there fast enough."

"Gregoire tends to be overprotective of his wife at times."

"'Unnaturally possessive' are the words I'd use to describe him. Where I come from, men don't treat their wives like chattels."

"This isn't America, Diana," he was quick to point out, "and from what you've told me about your own marriage, you're in no position to be criticizing any man for treating his wife with a good deal more respect and affection than your husband ever showed you. I'm sorry if Gregoire seemed distant, but things aren't always as they seem, and it so happens that he learned from bitter experience that it pays to be cautious with strangers."

"Well, he's got nothing to fear from me. I like Jeanne very much and certainly wish her no harm. We were having a lovely visit, until he came on the scene."

"If you say so."

"I do. Now, if you're done with the third-degree, I'd like to go to my room."

"By all means."

She gestured imperiously at the floor plan. "And I'd like to take that with me. I've marked the tour route on it, and made a few notes—all perfectly innocent, in case you're wondering!— that I need to study."

"Of course." Carefully he smoothed the curled edges of the paper flat before handing it over, then stepped aside. "I'll expect you for cocktails at seven, in the family drawing room. As I mentioned earlier, we dress for dinner here. I hope that doesn't present a problem for you?"

"Relax, Anton! I'll be there, appropriately clad. Despite

the impression I might have given, not all Americans are Neanderthals." Color still high with indignation, she swept past him.

"And I'm not a complete fool," he murmured under his breath, watching as she disappeared into her suite, and wondering what her reaction would be if she'd realized he'd taken a good look at her notes before returning them to her. "I made it clear the east wing's off-limits, so why, if you're the innocent you claim to be, did you see fit to circle a big question mark over it?"

Troubled on a number of fronts, he ran his fingers over his jaw. By her account, she and Gregoire had taken an instant dislike to one another. But Anton had known Gregoire Delancie nearly all his life, worked closely with him for more than eleven years, and in all that time the man had made only one error in judgment. That had been right after Marie-Louise's death, when he'd inadvertently said more than he should to the tabloid hunters swarming around the place.

If he'd picked up on something about the lovely Diana that didn't ring true, it bore investigation. He wasn't a man to take an irrational dislike to someone without cause.

The ping of fine crystal and murmur of voices led Diana to the family drawing room. Arriving unnoticed, she paused a moment on the threshold to survey the scene, and her immediate reaction was one of relief that she'd packed a couple of semi-formal dresses among her outfits.

For a start, the sheer magnificence of the room itself merited nothing less than the best from its occupants. All graceful curving walls, tall mullioned windows swagged in silk, and sparkling chandelier sconces, it filled the entire circumference of the west wing's second floor.

Anton stood at a carved library table, pouring champagne into wafer thin flutes. Sophie, glamorous in a clinging scarlet dress whose plunging neckline revealed an enviable amount of cleavage, perched on the arm of a nearby chair, swinging one long leg negligently and practically devouring him with her eyes. Not that Diana could blame her. In a black pin-striped suit, white shirt and burgundy tie, he looked good enough to eat.

The people who captured most of Diana's attention, however, were the two ladies she assumed to be Anton's aunts. In their late sixties or early seventies, they sat close together on a lushly upholstered sofa, not far from where she stood. One wore classic black silk, the other green moire taffeta.

"We both know she's after his money," the green taffeta declared audibly, flinging a scornful glare across the room at Sophie.

"She's after his body, as well, but she won't be getting either if I have any say in the matter," the other one countered. "Anton went through enough with Marie-Louise. I'm not about to stand idly by and let this brazen trollop sink her hooks into him, just when he's ready to resume a normal life again."

The green taffeta nodded grimly. "Nor I, *ma sœur.*"

Realizing the conversation wasn't intended for an outsider's ears, Diana was on the point of making her presence known when Anton happened to catch sight of her. "Diana! How long have you been standing there?"

"Hardly any time at all," she said, flustered by his welcoming smile.

It wasn't fair. No man given to bouts of irrational bad temper had any business being blessed with such an abundance of charm. It undermined her ability to arm herself against him and made her regret having snapped at him when he'd accosted her before dinner.

"Well, don't stand there waiting for an invitation. Come on in and let me introduce you to my aunts. They've been hopping with impatience to meet you." Leaving Sophie to her own devices, he drew Diana to where the two women turned to observe her with bright-eyed curiosity. "Aunt Hortense, Aunt Josette, this is Diana."

"Good evening, Diana, and welcome to the Château de Valois," Hortense, in the green taffeta, declared regally.

"Yes, welcome!" Josette echoed. "Anton told us about you, but he neglected to mention how young and pretty you are."

Too unfamiliar with titled aristocracy to know if she should address them individually as Madame la Comtesse, or even if they were Countesses to begin with, Diana opted for a safe, "Thank you, Mesdames de Valois. I'm very pleased to meet you."

"You have lovely manners, Diana. Such a rare thing among many young people, these days." Hortense shot a disapproving glance at Sophie. "But Mesdames de Valois is such a mouthful, let's dispense with the formalities. Just call us Aunt Hortense and Josette."

"And tell us about yourself." Josette patted the sofa's middle cushion. "All we know from Anton is that you're an American and you've volunteered to help out around here as tour guide this summer. What else about you is interesting and unusual?"

Anton rolled his eyes. "I'll serve the champagne," he said dryly. "I have a feeling you're going to need it, Diana."

"There's really not much else to tell," she confessed, accepting a seat between the aunts. "I'm here on holiday, speak French and can spare the time to lend a hand. That's about it."

"That's not it, at all!" Hortense shook a reproving finger. "We want to know about *you, cherie*. About your family, and where you live in America and where you went to school, and what kind of career you have."

Sophie drifted over and arranged herself in an armchair. "I'd like to hear what you've got to say about that, too. Everyone has a past, *mademoiselle*. Tell us about yours. For example, are your parents French?"

"My parents are dead," she replied, wondering what prompted such a question. "And they were American."

"So who taught you to speak such excellent French?"

"*They* did."

"Then they must have lived in France at some point. No American I've ever come across has that fine an ear for our language, unless they've spent a lot of time here."

Suppressing a twinge of uneasiness at the covert hostility in Sophie's manner, Diana said, "If they did, it was before I was born. This is the first time I've visited France."

Not the exact truth, perhaps, but close enough to pass for a little white lie.

"The first time?" Sophie regarded her skeptically. "Then why on earth would you choose to come here?"

Diana flicked a glance at Anton, remembering he'd asked her pretty much the same thing, and found him watching her now, waiting to hear her answer. "Why not? From everything I've read, Provence is a popular destination for overseas visitors."

Sophie wrinkled her nose. "But why settle for a backwater place like Bellevue-sur-Lac, when St. Tropez, Cannes and Antibes are only a stone's throw away, and have so much more to offer?"

"Because it's a beautiful, tranquil area, and the complete opposite of what I'm used to," she replied, increasingly ticked off with the woman's unrelenting stream of questions. "Why do *you* come here?"

"Because I'm family."

"Barely," Hortense intervened. "And only when it suits your convenience. Stop harassing our guest, Sophie, and let her speak without interruption. Go on, *ma chère*."

"I really don't have anything else to say," Diana replied, so rattled by Sophie's pitbull tenacity that she was afraid she'd trip herself up and let slip something incriminating.

Until then, Anton had stationed himself by the fireplace, content to remain an observer, but at that point he broke his silence. "What Diana isn't saying is that she's been through a difficult time lately, and finds talking about it still very painful.

She came looking for a place to heal her bruised spirit, and found it here, and that's all there is to it. Isn't that right, Diana?"

The gaze he settled on her was filled with such straightforward commiseration that she had to look away. "Yes," she said, and wished it was the truth, because lying to him was becoming too painful to bear.

There was more to this man than his good looks and irresistible charm. He possessed what she now realized Harvey had never owned: an integrity, a strength, a nobility of character that had nothing to do with his aristocratic birthright.

Never mind that she'd met him only yesterday and would be gone from his life within a month. She knew she'd remember him the rest of her days. Knew, too, with an unwavering instinct, that if circumstances had been different, if she could have shed the subterfuge which had brought her here, she might have learned to love him more completely, more passionately, than she'd ever loved before.

Josette touched her hand. "Your heart is sore," she said softly, "but you've come to the right place. You will heal here, *cherie*. We will see to that."

Just as well the dinner gong sounded then. One more second, one more sympathetic word, and Diana would have burst into tears.

The weekend passed uneventfully. She didn't see much of Anton, except in the evenings, but the aunts more than made up for it and kept her entertained.

"You must see the estate and meet everyone," Josette decided on the Saturday, and off they went, with Hortense behind the wheel of a station wagon almost as decrepit as Diana's rental car.

"I love it," Hortense said, jolting the poor thing merrily over the dusty, rutted roads. "We've grown old together and understand one another."

During the next hour or so, Diana was introduced to the people who ran the olive mill, lavender distillery, gift shop and perfumery, all of which remained open to the public, seven days a week. Finally they drove to the winery. Gregoire wasn't there, which Diana didn't see as any great loss, but his second-in-command showed her the gleaming equipment in the sheds and took her on a private tour of the cellars, or *caves,* although the aunts declined to accompany them because "it's too cool down there for our old bones."

In between each stop, they regaled her with details of how they'd come to live at the château, a story Anton had touched on only briefly.

"Our brother had run this entire estate," Hortense explained. "At the time of his and his wife's death, I was studying anthropology in Ecuador."

"And I was in Sweden on an extended visit with an old school friend," Josette continued. "Of course, when we heard of the tragedy, we came home immediately. Anton needed us, and not for a moment did we hesitate about devoting ourselves to him. In time, we sent him away to school and eventually to university, in order for him to learn how to take over for his father. But how to safeguard his inheritance in the meantime?" She shrugged eloquently.

Again, Hortense picked up the thread of the story. "The thing is, you see, we knew nothing about running an estate this size. We muddled along as best we could, at the mercy of unscrupulous outsiders who almost ruined us. The château was in disrepair, the grapevines diseased, the lavender fields and olive groves untended.

"If we hadn't persuaded Gregoire and Jeanne to come and help us, I do believe we'd have lost everything. Jeanne brought some sort of order to the running of the household, and Gregoire took over as chief vintner—he has 'the nose' required to run a successful winery. But willing though they were, they were but two people, and couldn't work miracles."

"Then, one day, Anton came home again, a man, and everything changed. He took charge," Josette declared, all puffed up with pride. "The village was dying, with more people in the church graveyard than walking the streets. To men and women alike, he gave life and hope and employment. Every day, from dawn to dusk, he worked beside them wherever he was needed—in the vineyards, the fields, at the château. He directed them in repairing the machinery, the buildings, the house."

"In short," Hortense concluded, "*Château de Valois et Cie* became the engine that drives the economy of Bellevue-sur-Lac. It's no wonder people here credit Anton with saving their lives and will go to any lengths to protect him."

Protect? The word struck an odd note to Diana's ears. Why would a man so highly esteemed need protection? She could hardly put the question to his aunts, though. He was clearly their hero.

Sunday was so warm and pleasant that, after dinner, they all took coffee on the terrace. The moon swam high, throwing dense shadows across the landscape. Romantic songs from the 1950s filtered from the drawing room, where Josette had loaded a stack of old vinyl LPs on the stereo turntable.

"They take me back to my youth," she said, swaying dreamily in the arms of an imaginary partner, the handkerchief hem of her purple chiffon dress whispering around her ankles. "Oh, to be in love again!"

"Oh, to be spared such maudlin rubbish," Sophie muttered.

"Do you like to dance, Diana?" Josette called, still twirling with her invisible partner to the soulful accompaniment of Edith Piaf singing *Je ne Regrette Rien*.

"Of course she does," Hortense scoffed. "You've only to look at her to know she was the most popular girl in her crowd."

"No, I wasn't," Diana had to admit. "I was shy, too smart in class and not particularly good at sports. As a teenager, I'd be the girl no boy asked to dance. I'd sit by myself and smile and pretend I was having a good time but inside I was bleeding."

"But you'll dance with me now, Diana," Anton said, and without waiting for an answer, took her hand and drew her to her feet.

The paving stones were uneven beneath her feet, but he held her so securely, she might have been floating on polished marble.

"Do you know why none of those boys asked you dance?" he murmured against her hair. "Because you were too beautiful, too fine, too unattainable. But in their hearts, you were the belle of the ball. The prize they all longed to win."

Don't talk like that, she begged silently, dazzled by a rush of pleasure that left her blood singing. *You make it too easy for me to fall in love with you.*

"That was lovely to see," Hortense sighed, when the song ended and Anton led Diana back to her chair. "So romantic, just the way it used to be, before we all forgot there *is* such a thing as romance. Don't you agree, Anton?"

"I do," he said. "What about you, Diana?"

She looked up to find him watching her intently, and her flesh burned under his gaze; burned in places that had lain cool and untouched for far too long. How was it that, with a single glance, he could bring her alive again? Remind her that she was a woman with a woman's needs, a woman's hunger?

Embarrassed by her body's responses, hidden, thank heaven, from his all-too-observant gaze, she cleared her throat and managed a noncommittal shrug.

Making no secret of her contempt for such unsophisticated entertainment, Sophie helped herself to more cognac. "All this harking back to the good old days is enough to drive a person to drink."

"Well, we won't have to worry about driving you," Josette

informed her sharply. "From the amount of alcohol you manage to put away every night, I'd say you're already there."

You took the words right out of my mouth, Diana thought. Sophie was so spiteful at times, she wanted to pinch her.

It wasn't until the next night, though, that she realized just how thoroughly hateful Anton's cousin could be.

The evening started out much as usual with the usual beautifully prepared five-course meal. The difference was that Jeanne came to supervise serving it, and witnessing her mother in the role of domestic, while she herself was treated like royalty, cut Diana to the quick. Not that Anton or his aunts were in the least overbearing toward Jeanne. Rather, they were warm and relaxed and very appreciative of her contribution to the evening, as well as that of the young maid working with her.

"Thanks for helping out tonight, Jeanne," Anton said, as she wheeled in the main course. "You put in enough hours during the day, without having to give up your evenings as well."

"Don't give it a second thought," she told him cheerfully. "I'm happy to lend a hand. Corinne's still nursing a migraine, and Odette's too new at the job to manage on her own."

"Well, please give Corinne our best, and tell her we hope she'll feel better soon."

"I will," she promised, and moved on to give quiet encouragement to the nervous young maid trying to fill up the water goblets without spilling a drop.

Sophie, on the other hand, appeared completely unfamiliar with the words "thank you," and seemed to think it was beneath her dignity to acknowledge the presence of anyone not actually seated at the table. When the subject of Henri's birthday party came up, she didn't even bother to wait until Jeanne had left the room before saying, "I hope we're not expected to take part in this bucolic celebration."

"You're more than welcome to stay away," Hortense replied,

"but we will certainly put in an appearance, and I hope that you, Diana, will join us."

"I wouldn't miss it," she said, miserably aware from her heightened color that Jeanne had heard Sophie's disparaging comment. "Henri treated me very kindly during the short time I stayed at the inn."

"I'm not surprised." Hortense smiled knowingly. "He's a very good-hearted man."

But Sophie, oblivious to Anton's black glare, was determined to have the last word. "I don't see what that's got to do with it. The fact is, he's a working-class individual and has nothing in common with people like us."

"*I* work for a living, Sophie," Anton pointed out, as Jeanne ushered the maid from the room. "Does that put me beyond your social pale, too?"

"Don't be silly, *cher*," she cooed. "You're merely managing your assets, which is a different thing entirely."

"No doubt you see your exhaustive search for another rich husband in the same redeeming light," Hortense remarked, which set Josette's long dangling earrings to taking on a life of their own as she tried to stifle a laugh.

Even Anton was hard-pressed not to smile. "All right, no more wine for you, Hortense," he scolded, the severity he tried to inject into his voice belied by the amusement dancing in his eyes.

"At my age, my dear nephew, a woman does what she must to survive the moment, and if that means getting plastered once in a while, well so be it," she retorted blithely, which practically put her sister under the table.

"The other event coming up, of course, is the Lavender Ball," Josette sputtered, when she managed to control herself. "I do so look forward to that. You'll enjoy it very much, Diana. We hold it here at the château, on the third Saturday in August. It's one of the few times the ballroom's used anymore, although when I was a young girl, there always seemed to be some grand occasion taking place."

"I'm not sure I'll still be here then," Diana said.

"Of course you will," Hortense decreed. "Three years is long enough to observe mourning, and it's past time Anton had a pretty woman on his arm again. If you don't have an evening gown, Josette and I will take you shopping in Nice."

And that was when the evening turned into a complete disaster. Jeanne and Odette had come back to the dining room to clear away the main course. Still smarting from having been put in her place by Hortense, Sophie vented her annoyance on poor Odette who had the misfortune to let the fork slide off Sophie's plate and into her lap.

If the hapless maid had deliberately emptied a glass of water over her head, Sophie couldn't have been more outraged. "What the *hell* kind of people do you have working for you, Anton?" she exploded.

"Calm down, Sophie. It was an accident," he said quietly.

Hurrying to the rescue with a clean linen napkin, Jeanne murmured, "I'm very sorry, *madame*. I'll take care of your dress and have it dry-cleaned in the morning."

"If you take care of it the way you train your maids," she snapped, slapping aside Jeanne's efforts with the back of her hand, "I don't want you within a mile of it, or me."

Diana saw the flash of anger in her mother's eyes. Saw how she opened her mouth to defend herself, then closed it again and averted her gaze. And she couldn't stand it.

"Don't speak to Jeanne like that," she said sharply.

Sophie sent her a poisonous glare. "It's none of your business how I choose to speak to the servants, Mademoiselle Reeves."

"I'm making it my business, Mademoiselle Beauvais," she shot back. "And unlike those you so carelessly dismiss as 'servants,' I'm free to tell you exactly what I think of your appalling lack of sensitivity. I don't know who taught you your manners, but they made a lousy job of it."

"Well said, Diana," Hortense murmured approvingly. "I couldn't have put it better myself."

Ignoring her, Sophie directed another blast at Diana. "Just who do you think you're speaking to?"

"Someone not fit to clean—!" *My mother's shoes, you unfeeling bitch!*

She stopped short, appalled at how close she'd come to letting slip a truth not hers to reveal. Sophie, though, wasn't inclined to let the matter drop.

"What?" she taunted. "Don't stop now. Speak your mind and have done with."

Chest heaving, Diana took a deep, shuddering breath. It managed to dampen her fury, but couldn't stem the tears that filled her eyes. Throwing down her napkin, she pushed herself away from the table. "Never mind! You're not worth spit, let alone the energy it takes to reason with you," she choked, and knew she had to leave before she said something she'd really live to regret.

The dining room was long, a mile or more it seemed, as she stumbled to the door at the far end, leaving behind a babble of voices. Josette's, sharp and critical, directed at Sophie. Hortense's joining in, blistering with anger. Anton's deep and forbidding, commanding order out of chaos. Odette weeping, and Jeanne's gentle tones dispensing comfort to the girl.

Dear God! Diana thought, fleeing up the stairs to her suite. What have I started with my insatiable need to find my mother? Why didn't I listen to Carol when she warned me nothing good could come of this? How will I ever face Anton again?

She didn't have to wait long to find out. Hadn't even made it as far as her door, in fact, before she heard his footsteps racing to catch up with her. "Diana, wait!" he said, his hands closing over her shoulders and putting an end to her blind dash to escape him.

"Go away," she cried, knowing how she must look, with her face all blotchy, and streaked with mascara, and squinched up like a wrinkled old apple. She'd humiliated herself enough for one night, without him seeing her like this.

"No," he said. "Not until you tell me what set you off back there."

"Isn't it obvious? Your benighted cousin is about as pleasant as a blood clot, and since you didn't see fit to tell her so, I did it for you."

"That's not what I'm talking about. I was watching your face, long before you opened fire on her. There's something else going on here, something that troubles you deeply, and I want to know what it is."

"I can't..." She was sobbing openly now. "I can't talk about it, not tonight."

"All right," he said quietly, after a lengthy pause. "All right."

Then guiding her through her door and closing it firmly behind him, he took her in his arms and let her cry. She sank against him, borrowing his strength. Wishing it was hers to keep forever. He smoothed her hair. Ran his hands up and down her back; long, soothing strokes meant to comfort.

At what point did it all change? When did she lift her face to his, knowing that he couldn't mistake the naked need in her eyes? When did his lips stop murmuring words of reassurance and, instead, settle softly on hers? Most of all, how did a kiss that started out as a fleeting benediction evolve into a hot, greedy, openmouthed confession of desire?

She had no answers. Knew no truths but the one her body had recognized practically from the first. Her hands stole up around his neck. Closing her eyes, she let her head fall back in tacit surrender as his mouth traveled a path from her jaw to her throat.

His fingers slid up her rib cage and rested cool against her bare skin as he pushed aside the broad straps of her dress. He kissed her shoulder, her collarbone. Delicately. With restrained finesse. Flirting with her breasts, but never quite touching them. Until she was so hungry for him that she whimpered and begged him not to stop.

"Are you sure?" he asked, his voice rough with passion.

"Oh, yes," she gasped.

There was no restraint, after that. Sweeping her off her feet as if she weighed next to nothing, he strode through her little sitting room to her bedroom and set her on her feet again.

With nothing but a Provence moon glimmering through the window to guide him, he found the zipper at the back of her dress, the clasp holding closed her bra. Dropping to his knees, he peeled away her silk stockings, and then, as if he couldn't deny himself a moment longer a taste of what was to come, he put his mouth on the satin triangle of her panties.

She felt his tongue swirling against her, his hands reaching up to caress her breasts, and a lightning bolt flashed the length of her. Her thighs trembled. Her knees buckled.

He caught her before she fell, and eased her onto the bed. Looked down at her. Shaped with his hands the curve of her hip, the dip of her waist, the slope of her breast. Touched her between her legs, lightly, deliberately. And when she arched off the mattress with a sharp cry, he stripped off his own clothes, yanking impatiently at the knot in his tie, ripping open the buttons on his shirt. His shoes landed with a thud on the floor, his cuff links flew through the air, shooting streaks of silver in the night.

She caught a brief, moon-washed glimpse of his naked body. The planes of his chest, the width of his shoulders. His flat stomach, his long, strong legs…and *it,* jutting big and hard and powerful from the dark nest of his pubic hair. The breath caught in her throat. He was magnificent.

She opened her arms and he came to her, burying her under his weight and entered her in one long, smooth thrust that rocked her soul. Effortlessly he swept her with him on a mounting wave of passion that turned the familiar into something far, far beyond the range of her previous experience. No hurried, pedestrian exercise this, with him spent and satisfied in minutes, and her straining to find a release which always eluded her. This, she thought dazedly, as the distant ripples of orgasm intensified in the deepest part of her, was not sex, it was ecstasy. It was sharing and caring and joy.

And when, with a moan that ripped her in two, she climaxed at the same time that he did, it was much more than that. It was love.

After, when he rolled to his side and cradled her in his arms, may God forgive her, she thought, just for a second, of Harvey. "It's got nothing to do with size," he used to bluster. "It's knowing what to do with it that counts."

She smiled into the warm curve of Anton's neck. Poor Harvey. He really didn't have a clue—on either point!

CHAPTER SEVEN

Of course, the euphoria didn't last. Like a man waking from a very bad dream, Anton eventually stirred and, with a great sigh, swung his legs over the side of the bed. "*Mon dieu!* What have I done?" he muttered, burying his head in his hands.

A chill crept over Diana as all the lovely warmth seeped from her body. She ached to touch him; to lay her hand against the smooth skin of his back, and say, "You just taught me what making love is all about."

But he'd cloaked himself in distance. Was already rooting around in the dark for his clothes and climbing into them with insulting haste. She'd have been crushed, if she hadn't been too numb with shock to feel much of anything.

Not about to let him know how humiliated she was, she reached out and flicked on the bedside lamp. By then, he had on his trousers and was buttoning his shirt, although he'd not yet tucked in the latter. "There," she said. "That should help. If you hurry, you might still make it back to the dining room in time for dessert."

He stared at her as if he thought she'd lost her mind. "Are you all right, Diana?"

No, she wanted to scream at him. *I ache in places I didn't know existed. I'm still throbbing inside from the explosion of an orgasm the likes of which, until tonight, I've only ever read about. Thanks to you, I'll never be the same again.* "What do you want me to say, Anton?"

"Something other than a glib remark about a missed course at dinner, certainly! What just happened between us...shouldn't have. I'm not in the habit of jumping into bed with someone I've known little more than a week, and nor, I think, are you."

"True. But we can't turn back the clock. What's done, is done."

"*Pour l'amour de dieu,* woman, you could be pregnant!"

Oh, if only! To have not just a child, but *his* child! To hold his son to her breast, to touch his baby-soft skin, and smell his baby-sweet scent...! Her heart clenched at the thought. "It's a bit late in the day to think about that, wouldn't you say?"

He groaned and tunneled his fingers through his hair. "Damn you, anyway! You bewitched me."

"It took two, Anton. Don't lay all the blame on me. You're the one who followed me upstairs. You're the one who decided you had the right to come inside my suite. I didn't invite you in."

"You didn't kick me out, either."

She fell back against the pillows, all the fight going out of her. "No, I didn't," she said, hollow with pain. "What kind of a fool does that make me?"

He scooped up his tie, retrieved one of his cuff links and gave up on finding the other. "This is pointless. As you say, what's done is done. We have no choice now but to deal with the consequences."

"Well, if you're worried I'm going to try to rope you into a shotgun wedding, don't be," she said. "That's more your cousin Sophie's style than mine. Even if I did find myself pregnant, I wouldn't ask you for anything. I have the resources to look after myself *and* a child, if I have to."

"And if you think for one moment that a child of mine is going to grow up not knowing his father, you're sadly mistaken!"

"Oh, go away, and stop trying to intimidate me," she sighed wearily. "Quite apart from the fact that you don't want me in your life, and I wouldn't let you take my baby out of mine, we're anticipating problems that might never arise. Go back to your dinner party and tell your aunts I have a headache. It won't be a complete lie."

"I have no more appetite for a dinner party than you have," he replied stonily. "But you're right. There's nothing to be gained by our continuing this conversation now. We will talk later, when cooler heads prevail."

Like hell we will! she almost said. *I'm out of here, first thing tomorrow, and nothing you can say or do is going to stop me.*

But that wasn't true, she realized, even as the thought took shape in her mind. She'd come to the château for one reason only: to substantiate her belief that Jeanne was her mother and establish some sort of permanent connection with her, no matter how tenuous it might be. Until she'd achieved that goal, nothing and no one was going to chase her away.

Quite how she'd face Anton during that time was another matter entirely. But she'd find a way. She had to.

She was late coming down the next morning. When she finally appeared, she seemed composed, but the smudges under her eyes attested to how poorly she'd slept.

"How are you feeling, *ma petite?*" Josette wanted to know.

"I've been better," she admitted.

"We're so sorry about last night."

Her glance flickered to him, and shied away again. "I'm the one who should apologize. I'm afraid I created quite a scene."

"No, Diana," Hortense said. "You put an end to a scene not of your making, and you did it in fine fashion. Help yourself to some breakfast, *ma chère.* You'll feel better after you've eaten."

Anton watched as, avoiding his gaze, she went to the sideboard where the usual selection of fresh fruit, rolls and coffee was laid out. Last night, she'd worn silk that had whispered under his hands, beguiling him to slide it down her body. Today, she'd chosen a navy skirt and white cotton blouse.

So proper, he thought, watching her moodily as she buttered a roll. *So restrained. Who'd guess her capable of the fire burning under that prim, nunlike outfit?*

He wished he could forget. Had paced the floor most of the night, trying to erase the memory of the taste and scent and feel of her. But more than that, he'd struggled to empty his mind of the way she'd responded to him. Wild with passion. Uttering desperate little cries. Shattering around him. The polar opposite of poor, driven Marie-Louise whose sole reason for intercourse had nothing to do with desire.

Setting down his coffee cup, he rose abruptly from the table. "I need to go over a few things with you when you're done here, Diana," he said tersely. "I'll be in my office. By now, you know where to find it. Please don't keep me waiting any longer than necessary."

He felt his aunts' astonished stares following him as he strode from the room, and knew they were taken aback by the brusque arrogance of his tone. How much more horrified they'd be, if they learned that the reason for it sprang from his sense of deep personal shame. *Droit du seigneur* had not been part of their teaching when they'd instructed him on his role as the most recent Comte de Valois, and never mind that Diana wasn't a virgin. That he'd taken advantage of her when she was at her most vulnerable was almost as bad.

She showed up at his office twenty minutes later. Time enough for him to rehearse what he knew he had to say. "Thank you for coming," he began, closing the door.

"I wasn't aware I'd been given any choice in the matter," she said stonily.

He pulled forward a chair. "Please, Diana, sit down and hear me out."

Mouth set in a stubborn line, she perched on the edge of her seat, ready to take flight at the slightest provocation. Resuming his place behind his desk, he watched her a moment, trying to determine what thoughts lay hidden behind her pale, lovely face. Finally he said, "First of all, I need to ask—have I made it impossible for you to remain here?"

She looked down at her fingers which lay knotted in her lap. "I don't know. I'm still trying to decide."

Encouraged that she hadn't handed him a flat, *Yes, you unfeeling bastard!* he nodded. "Then before you do, let me say this. I assume full responsibility for what took place between us last night. I was wrong and can offer no excuse for the way I behaved."

"The whole incident could have been avoided, if you'd spoken up at the dinner table, instead of leaving it to me."

"You hardly gave me the chance."

"That cousin of yours needs to be taught a lesson."

"And I'll deal with her in a way she won't forget, never fear that. But right now, I'm more concerned about you—and us."

"There isn't any 'us.'"

"There might be, and that's the other reason I needed to speak to you in private as soon as possible. Diana, I want your solemn promise that if you find yourself pregnant, you'll tell me immediately. I say this not to threaten or coerce you in any way, but because I have an obligation to the mother of my child that I cannot and will not ignore."

"If, by that, you're suggesting we get married—"

"I'm suggesting nothing. I'm asking for your promise to keep me informed. How we proceed from there, should the situation in fact arise, is something we'll decide together, but it would be premature on both our parts to assume that marriage is the only course open to us. We are strangers."

"Who've been intimate with one another." She shook her head, whether in disgust or despair, he couldn't tell.

"Yes." He let a beat of silence pass before phrasing the

question he felt compelled to ask. "Is it likely, do you think, that you could have conceived?"

"I don't know the answer to that. My ex-husband was so against our having children that he was very careful not to risk producing any—at least, not with me. How easily I could conceive…" She shrugged. "I guess that remains to be seen."

"Then let me put it this way. Are you at that stage of your monthly cycle when a woman is most likely to conceive?"

She blushed. "That's a very personal question, don't you think?"

"It's a very *relevant* question, given the circumstances."

"And where exactly is it written that, just because you're the Comte de Valois, you're entitled to access the private details of my life?"

"Answer the question, Diana."

The hunted glance she cast around the room confirmed his worst fears even before she opened her mouth to deliver a stark, "Yes."

"Then if you *are* pregnant, we'll know within a week or two."

"I suppose." She slapped the arms of her chair and glared at him. "Is that it? May I leave now?"

"Not until you tell me what prompted your outburst to my cousin, last night, and don't bother passing it off as a spur-of-the-moment impulse. You'd been biting your tongue from the moment we sat down at the table."

"I'm American," she said. "We don't 'do' class systems in our society. Household staff aren't treated as if they're a lower form of life. Poor Odette was so terrified, she was shaking."

"Yet you seemed more upset at the way my cousin responded to Jeanne."

"I was. I've told you before, I like Jeanne very much, and it made me sick to see a woman her age having to take such shabby treatment from someone young enough to be her daughter."

"Well, not quite that young, Diana, unless Jeanne gave birth when she was still a child herself!" he said, and wondered why the color rode up her face a second time. "But I see your point. What *you* perhaps don't see, though, is that Jeanne was more disturbed by your behavior than she was by Sophie's. However well meant, your reaction put the spotlight on her and made a bad situation worse. I suggest that the next time you decide to take my cousin to task, you do so privately."

"There won't be a next time," she informed him. "I'll be eating my meals with the rest of the *hired help,* in future."

"Do that, and you'll be making exactly the kind of class distinction you accuse me of tolerating. And that, I promise you, will make Jeanne far more uncomfortable than anything my illmannered cousin metes out."

"Oh, that's the last thing I want! She might be just the housekeeper to you, but I'd be proud to call her my…friend."

"She's a lot more than just a housekeeper to me, Diana. She's been my friend since I was a boy. A second mother, even. We just play by slightly different rules here from what you're used to in America, that's all."

He saw how she struggled to come to terms with what he'd said. The way she pressed her lips together, the sigh she couldn't suppress, the very real distress in her eyes were impossible to miss. At last, on yet another sigh, she muttered, "All right, you've made your point. As long as I'm living under your roof, I suppose I must do things your way. When in Provence, and all that…"

If only I could be sure you mean it, Diana, he thought, *how much easier it would be for me to trust you—and how much more difficult I'd find it to stay out of your bed!*

Wrenching his outrageous thoughts under control with difficulty, he said, "Then let's put the matter to rest and get down to business. The tours start tomorrow and include the wine cellar, which you've yet to learn about, so I've arranged for Gregoire to show you around and explain what you need to know."

Her face fell. "Why him?"

"Because he's the wine expert around here and the best person for the job." *And I don't trust myself to be alone with you, most especially not in a dimly lit and cloistered space.*

"Well, if I must…"

"It'll be painless, Diana, I promise."

She tilted one shoulder dismissively, and he wished she hadn't. The soft rise and fall of her breasts were more than his libido could handle with equanimity. "If you say so. Is there anything else?"

"Non," he said, doing his damnedest to ignore the blood surging in his groin. *"C'est tout—pour le moment."*

"C'est tout." Gregoire Delancie brushed one hand against the other. "That's all, *madame.* Do you have any questions?"

"None that I can think of," she said, heading for the cellar's massive oak door, as anxious to be rid of his company as he undoubtedly was of hers. "You've been very helpful. I'll study your notes, and if I run across any problems, I'll let you know."

"Then just one more thing before you leave, *s'il vous plait.*"

"Yes?" She turned back and caught the oddest look on his face.

"What's your interest in my wife?"

Goose bumps that had nothing to do with the cellar's chill raced over her skin. Why would he put such a question to her? What did he think he knew? "I'm not sure I understand the question."

"You seem to be making a point of singling her out for your attention. I'm wondering why."

"If you're referring to us having tea together—"

"That, and the incident at dinner, last night."

"Jeanne told you about it?"

"Certainly. I am her husband. Of course she confided in me. Why would you, a stranger, feel compelled to interfere in a situation that in no way involved you?"

"She's a very nice woman and I didn't like the way she was being treated. Isn't that reason enough?"

"Why don't you tell me, Madame Reeves?" he said.

"I don't owe you any explanations, Monsieur Delancie."

"That is true. But in the interest of fair play, allow me to offer a warning to you. Jeanne is a kind and trusting soul who takes people at face value until they give her reason not to. I, however, am less inclined to be so charitable, and instinct tells me that you, young lady, are not quite as you'd like us all to believe. I don't pretend to understand why this is so, but let me make it very clear that if, for whatever the reason, you hurt my wife in any way, you'll answer to me."

Flabbergasted, she said, "You seem to be confusing me with the other guest in the house, Monsieur Delancie. I'm not the one who treated your wife like dirt, and I have absolutely no interest in causing her any kind of grief at all, *ever!*"

"I'd like to think you're telling me the truth."

"I am," she said shortly. "And if you choose not to believe me, that's your problem, not mine."

For a moment, he almost smiled, and she thought she saw a grudging respect in his eyes before he schooled his features into their usual grim impassivity. "You're a spirited woman, Madame Reeves," he remarked ambiguously, and held open the door for her.

And you're a jerk! she thought, stalking past him. *Why in the world would my mother marry a man like you?*

The week following passed, for the most part, in a blur of tourists peppering her with questions, her fielding answers and hoping she had her facts straight, and parents letting their children dart under the ropes barring entry to the different rooms, or, worse yet, losing track of them altogether in the gardens. By the Friday, though, as her familiarity with the château and its history increased, she'd grown more comfortable in her role and more confident in her dealings with the public.

The remaining days of the month formed a pattern in which

her intensive hours of work were offset by interludes of utter relaxation. Each morning before breakfast, she swam in the pool. After the last tour of the day, she lounged on the terrace, reading or visiting with the aunts. They showered her with affection, made her laugh with their witty observations and generally went out of their way to treat her as if she were one of their own.

Even Sophie made a grudging effort to be pleasant, largely, Diana suspected, because Hortense and Josette wouldn't give her the time of day, and she had no one else to talk to until the evening, when Anton usually put in an appearance.

Diana's skin turned honey-colored from the sun, and the sharp protrusion of her hips and collarbone, legacy of her marriage breakdown, softened into curves as a result of the wonderful menus her mother organized. Without being too obvious about it, she reinforced their budding friendship whenever the opportunity arose, sometimes with a compliment on a particular dish, sometimes just in passing the time of day when they happened to run into one another about the house. As far as Diana was concerned, no occasion was too brief or insignificant to be wasted, and seeing her mother's face light up at the sight of her gave her spirits a lift that nothing could dampen.

Well, almost nothing. Counting the hours until her next period was due, and trying to bury the ache in her heart whenever she let her thoughts stray to Anton, cast a cloud on even the sunniest day. Try though she might, she couldn't forget his touch, his kisses, or the way he'd filled her with his passion and vigor.

Of course, it wasn't love. How could it be when, as he'd so succinctly put it, "We are strangers"? But whatever it was she felt for him neither went away nor diminished, but raged in her blood with inexhaustible appetite.

It was just as well that she saw him only in the evenings, and always with other people present. At least that way, she had to keep her emotions in check. Even so, she found her glance repeatedly settling on his face, so compelling in its spare, aristocratic beauty. Caught herself committing to memory how his mouth moved when he spoke, how he used his hands to illustrate a point in conversation.

He watched her, too. But not for the same infatuated reason. *Well?* his eyes would ask, his gaze locking with hers.

It's too soon to tell, she'd radio back.

And his aunts, missing nothing and misinterpreting everything, would nod to one another and exchange satisfied smiles that said, *They're falling for each other! Let's start planning the wedding!*

It isn't what you think, she wanted to tell them.

And it wasn't. It was worse because, as the second week in July dragged to a close, Diana was forced to recognize that she could no longer pretend time was on her side. Even though it frequently felt imminent, her period did not happen. Instead other changes took its place. Her breasts grew tender and felt fuller. She was unusually tired all the time and experiencing the need to urinate frequently. Certain smells made her queasy—coffee, for instance, which she loved.

Meanwhile, the countdown to Henri's birthday party, scheduled for the following Saturday, clicked into high gear. As she understood it, friends and relatives were preparing trays of ratatouille and other vegetable dishes. His youngest brother, who was also the village butcher, had ordered a suckling pig for roasting on a spit over a bed of coals on the beach.

The baker had hauled out his molding machine and made dozens of *Caissons d'Aix,* little boat-shaped pastries which he filled with almond paste and topped with sugar icing. Anton was donating the wine. Jeanne and her staff were baking a cake large enough to feed a hundred guests.

Just hearing about it all was enough to give Diana the heaves and send her to bed for a long nap. When the Saturday dawned hot and sunny, she debated pleading a headache and begging off attending, but since everyone, from the latest newborn to Anton and the aunts, would be there, this was one occasion when no one would think it strange to see the Count's American visitor socializing freely with his housekeeper, and that wasn't an opportunity to be passed up lightly.

"Anton's filled the Range Rover with wine and folding chairs, and doesn't have room for a passenger, so you'll drive to the lake with us," Hortense decreed, after breakfast. "Gregoire will bring the car around at eleven."

Oh, yes, her mother's ever-vigilant, obsessively possessive husband! Diana had done her best to forget about him although, to be fair, he'd been civil enough, the few times she'd seen him since the day he'd shown her around the wine cellar. So, wearing a loose-fitting dress of gauzy white Indian cotton, and red, flat-heeled sandals, she dutifully showed up at five minutes to the hour, a camera tucked in her bag. She intended taking as many photographs of Jeanne as possible, just in case they were all she had to remember her mother by, after she left France.

Hortense and Josette were already ensconced in the back seat of a vintage Pierce Arrow convertible sedan, the likes of which would have stopped traffic had it rolled down any street in the U.S., but which seemed perfectly at home in the timeless serenity of rural Provence.

The party was well underway by the time they arrived. Henri, wearing a smile that wouldn't go away, sat in the place of honor, surrounded by some of his extended family. Others clustered around the fire pit while their wives kept an eye on long, cloth-covered tables that groaned under a mountain of food. Young mothers sat in the shade with babies on their laps, watching their male counterparts kick around a soccer ball. Children splashed in the warm waters of the lake.

Her uncles, her cousins, her aunts—and her mother, coming

to where Diana, fighting off a wave of nausea, stood apart from the crowd.

"You're looking pale, Diana. Is the heat too much for you? May I bring you something cold to drink?"

"Water," she managed to say, swallowing the saliva pooling in her mouth.

Alert as always to his wife's whereabouts and doings, Gregoire joined them. "This is your brother's day, *mon amour.* Be with him and leave me to take care of Madame Reeves."

"Actually I think I'm going to take a walk, so I really don't need either of you to take care of me," Diana insisted faintly.

Gregoire eyed her critically, then took her arm in a surprisingly gentle grip. "Jeanne's right. You don't look well, *madame.* Perhaps you need to eat something."

Her stomach lurched. "Oh, no…!"

But he ushered her to the tables anyway. Trays of sliced tomatoes sprinkled with oregano and swimming in oil gazed up at her…fat green olives and purple aubergine and anchovies and pickled eel. Gagging, she turned aside, and came face-to-face with the suckling pig rotating on the spit, fat hissing and spitting and running down its carcass.

"Madame, I am concerned. I think you should sit down."

"No! Please, Gregoire…!" Desperate to escape his watchful gaze, she pulled free and stumbled toward a stand of trees some distance away.

"Diana," she heard him call, but she kept going, her hand clamped across her mouth, until she could go no farther.

Bent double, she retched time and time again, her mouth filled with the sour, acidic taste of bile.

Anton ran her to earth not long after, and took one look at her as she leaned weakly against the trunk of a young pine tree, with her face bathed in sweat and her hair sticking to her scalp.

"Since we both know the reason, I won't insult my intelligence or yours by asking the cause of your sudden *maladie,*

Diana," he said, mopping her forehead with his handkerchief. "The only relevant questions are, how long have you known, and when were you planning to share the news with me?"

CHAPTER EIGHT

"DON'T start on me, Anton," she moaned, clutching at her midriff. "I'm not in the mood."

That much was obvious. She looked half-dead. "Is there anything I can do for you?"

She spared him an evil glare. "You've already done enough, thanks."

Well, he thought, he'd walked right into that one. "Look, Diana," he said patiently, "in your present condition, you're not helping anyone, least of all yourself, by trying to pick a fight you don't have a hope of winning, especially not with me."

"Oh, that's right! Nobody challenges the almighty Count de Valois, who ranks second only to God as far as everyone in these parts is concerned. Forgive me for having forgotten."

Foolish, stubborn creature! Her attempt to cut him to ribbons with sarcasm might have stood a better chance of finding its mark if she'd been able to deliver it without her chin quivering uncontrollably, and she hadn't been hanging on to the tree trunk for dear life because it was the only thing keeping her upright.

Recognizing it was pointless trying to reason with her, he left her alone with her misery and made his way back to the party. Apart from Gregoire, no one appeared to have missed him.

"You found her, Anton?"

"Yes. Thanks for the heads-up, Gregoire. You're right. She isn't well."

"What seems to be the trouble?"

"An upset stomach. Must be something she ate."

"I'm sorry. Is there anything I can do?"

"Yes." Anton handed him the keys to the Range Rover. "My car's in the public parking area, with everyone else's. Do me a favor, will you? Drive it down to this end and park it off the road, under the trees. That way, we can make a quiet exit and not spoil the party for others. And, Gregoire, if anyone asks, you haven't seen us."

"I understand. You can count on my discretion."

"I know it." He clapped the man on the back, took a bottle of mineral water from a nearby picnic hamper, and headed back into the wooded area again.

She was where he'd left her, except she was sitting at the base of the tree with her eyes closed, and her head resting against its trunk. Squatting down beside her, he uncapped the water. "Try a little of this. It might help."

Wordlessly she accepted the bottle, and took a few lethargic sips.

"Better?" he asked, when she was done.

"A little." She set down the bottle and expelled a weary sigh. "I'll be okay now. You can go back to the party."

"And leave you here? Don't be absurd. I'm taking you back to the château."

"I don't need you to take me anywhere," she said irritably. "Stop fussing, Anton! I can look after myself."

He took her hands firmly in his. "And I need you to understand that I'm not the enemy, Diana. You don't have to look after yourself. I'm here and I want to help you. We're in this together."

"No, we're not," she whispered, tears sparkling in her eyes again. "We had sex once, that's all."

"It would seem that once was enough."

She bit her lip and looked away in such despair that he wanted nothing more than to take her in his arms and comfort her. But the longer they lingered here, the greater the chance that they'd be discovered, and he wasn't ready to share with anyone else news he'd not yet had time to come to grips with, himself.

The familiar sound of his Range Rover slowing to a stop beyond the trees spurred him to action. *"Viens!"* he said, hoisting her to her feet and slipping an arm around her waist. "Lean on me, and let's get out of here."

Five minutes later, they were speeding back to the château and by the time they arrived, her color had improved. "Would you like to lie down and rest for a while?" he asked, guiding her inside the house.

"No." She shot him a weak smile. "The nausea's passed, and I'm feeling almost human again."

Maybe so, but she still looked as if a good wind would blow her over. "You'd feel better still if you ate something. The staff have been given the day off so there's no one in the kitchen, but the refrigerator will be well stocked and I can boil an egg and make a pot of coffee, if you like."

She shuddered delicately. "No egg, thanks, and no coffee. But I could probably manage some toast and tea."

"Go put your feet up then, and I'll get to it."

"For heaven's sake, Anton," she objected, shying away from him as if she thought he might toss her over his shoulder and force her into submission, "I'm pregnant, not paralyzed! I can make my own toast."

Willing to let her have her way, at least for now, he raised his hands in surrender. "Okay, then we'll both raid the kitchen. Toast and tea for you, and something a bit more substantial for me, since I'm missing out on all that good food down at the lake."

"There's no reason you have to miss out on anything. Go back to the party and have a good time."

"And how do I do that, Diana?" he asked wryly. "By pretending the last half hour didn't happen?"

"You might as well. Staying here isn't going to change anything."

"That is true, but there's a lot we need to talk about, and now's as good a time as any to get started."

"We can do that later."

"Non, ma chère," he contradicted her flatly, steering her down the corridor to the kitchen end of the house. "We do it now."

In the wake of her marriage breakdown, one thing Diana decided she'd never again tolerate was having her opinions dismissed as if they weren't worth the breath it took to utter them. But when Anton high-handedly ordered her to leave the preparation of their impromptu meal to him, she was glad enough to let him get on with it. She hadn't seen the kitchen before and, wandering to the far end of the room, she flopped down on a wide padded window seat, curious to learn more about her mother's domain.

The room was vast, with rough-hewn beams and white plaster walls that had been there since the château was first built. Essentially split into two areas, the working half contained streamlined luxury appliances and gleaming countertops that offered the ultimate in convenience and efficiency. But where she sat, the charm of French country furniture served as a reminder that even in a house this grand, the kitchen was more than just a place to cook meals. In many ways, it still represented the heart of the home.

A bouquet of roses and lavender, arranged in a yellow pitcher, graced the middle of an old farmhouse table, which was surrounded by rush-bottomed ladder-back chairs of the same vintage. A beautiful carved dresser stood against one wall, its open plate racks filled with colorful Provencal pottery.

Braids of garlic hung from the ceiling. Pots of herbs grew

on the windowsills. A black iron pot was suspended over the hearth in the big, brick fireplace. Ripe red tomatoes in a dark blue bowl made a splash of color against the white marble work surface of a center island.

If things had been different, she could have grown up here, playing with her dolls by the fire in winter, or sprawled on the window seat, reading, in the summer. She could have learned to walk on the tiled floor, stood on a chair and licked the spoon when her mother baked a cake. Sent letters to Santa Claus up the big open chimney. Opened gifts piled under a Christmas tree in the corner, and—

"Wake up, dreamer! Your toast and tea are ready."

Anton's voice put an end to her fantasy of a past that never was, and brought her back to a present altogether real and riddled with uncertainty. Joining him at the table, she nibbled at her toast while he dug into the cheese omelet he'd prepared for himself.

When the first pangs of hunger were satisfied, he put down his fork and said, "You're quite sure you're expecting a baby, are you, Diana?"

"Well, I can't give you proof positive, if that's what you mean," she conceded. "Pregnancy test kits aren't exactly thick on the ground around here, and since I'm presently without a car, I haven't been able to visit a pharmacy. But yes, I know enough about the early symptoms to be pretty certain that I am."

"Then we must see a doctor. We'll take care of it, first thing on Monday."

"We?"

"Of course, we! You don't suppose I'm leaving you to handle this on your own, do you?"

"I don't know," she said, afraid to let him see how badly she wanted to believe him. "Even though you've known all along that this might happen, it still must have come as a shock. It's hardly what you had planned, after all."

"Life's like that, sometimes. I've learned to cope with the

unexpected. And not to put too fine a point on it, but who else do you have to turn to?"

My mother, she thought, the pain of not being able to reveal herself to Jeanne more acute than usual. If ever there was a time when a woman needed her mother, it had to be when she was expecting her own first baby. Who better understood the fears, the doubts, the hopes? Who better able to offer reassurance and advice? But in this instance, Jeanne was relegated to the role of observer, with no idea that she was about to become a grandmother.

"You knew that before you met her," Carol had said the night before, when Diana had phoned and tearfully confided in her friend. "For now, let friendship be enough. At least then, you can keep your hopes alive that something better might evolve in the future. But spill the truth, and you could lose what little you have."

"What you're trying to say," she'd countered, "is that I still have no solid proof that Jeanne's really my mother."

"I know you want her to be, Diana, but wanting doesn't make it so, and it seems to me that you've got complications enough in your life enough right now, without adding more. The Diana I know would show more sense than to let herself be seduced by a man she barely knows, even if he is handsome as sin and an honest-to-goodness Count, as well. What in the world were you thinking?"

"Obviously I wasn't, or I wouldn't be in this mess, now. But that doesn't change how I feel about my mother."

"But what if you're wrong, and she isn't your mother? Think of the fall-out, if you start making allegations that aren't true about a woman your lover values so highly."

But Diana knew in her bones that she wasn't wrong. With every passing day, she grew more convinced of the blood tie between her and Jeanne. How else to account for the inexplicable emotional connection, the gut-level certainty, that tugged at her every time their eyes met?

"What the devil…?" Again, Anton interrupted her stream of thought, and startled by his tone, she looked up to find him poised to leap out of his chair, his head cocked attentively. Then she heard it, too: the sound of the outside service door quietly opening and footsteps approaching.

A moment later, Jeanne and Gregoire came into the kitchen, but stopped short at the sight confronting them.

"So sorry, Anton," Gregoire said, his glance taking in the eggshells, block of cheese and loaf of bread on the counter, and the frying pan on the stove. "We had no idea you'd be down here, and didn't mean to intrude."

"Why are you here at all?" he responded brusquely. "You're not due back until five o'clock."

"When Jeanne heard Madame Reeves wasn't feeling well and had returned to the château, she insisted on coming back too, in case she was needed."

So I'm Madame Reeves again, am I? Diana thought, remembering he'd called her by her first name, down by the lake.

Visibly annoyed, Anton said, "I thought I asked you to keep your mouth shut on the subject, Gregoire?"

"I did my best," he replied miserably, "but Jeanne had already spoken with Madame Reeves and knew something was amiss."

"That's true, Anton," Diana said, feeling almost sorry for the man. "Don't blame him, or Jeanne, for that matter. If anyone's at fault, I am. I knew I wasn't feeling up to par, and should have stayed home in the first place." She aimed a sympathetic smile at the worried couple. "But as you can see, I'm much better now, so the two of you should hurry back to your party before you, too, are missed."

"I'm afraid it's too late for that, Diana," Jeanne confessed. "When I realized you had disappeared, and I couldn't find my husband, I told Mesdames Hortense and Josette. They were worried enough that they didn't want to stay at the party, either."

Annoyed all over again, Anton blurted, "Are you saying you brought them back here, as well?"

"We had no choice," Gregoire replied. "They wouldn't have it any other way. Of course, when we dropped them off at the front door—"

"They spotted my car, and are probably prowling the halls, looking for us, even as we speak." He rolled his eyes in exasperation. "So much for keeping a low profile!"

Pushing back her chair, Diana urged him toward the door. "It can't be helped, Anton, and there's no real harm done. Let's just go find them and put their minds at rest. Jeanne, Gregoire, thank you for being so kind. I'm sorry I've spoiled the day for you, and for the mess we've made of your kitchen."

"Think nothing of it," her mother exclaimed. "We're just very relieved that you're feeling better. You looked so ill before, I was quite frightened for you."

Oh, Mother, if only I could explain that I'm not sick at all, how quickly your fear might turn to joy! Biting her lip, Diana paused in passing and squeezed Jeanne's hand. "Don't worry about me, Jeanne," she murmured huskily. "I'm really quite fine."

They met Hortense and Josette at the foot of the stairs in the grand hall. Less easily convinced that there was no need for worry, the aunts bombarded them with questions.

"Where were you? We've looked everywhere."

"Why didn't you let us know Diana wasn't well, instead of sneaking away without a word?"

"Have you called Dr. Savard, Anton?"

"Do you have a fever, Diana?"

"Are you in pain?"

"Shouldn't you be in bed?"

Finally Anton put a stop to the hullabaloo. "Enough, both of you! If Diana was unwell before, she has to be feeling a lot worse now, with all the fuss you're creating."

"That's easy for you to say," Josette scolded, "because, like most men, you see only what's under your nose, but we've noticed for several days now that Diana has looked peaked, and we have every right to make a fuss about it, if we choose. Someone has to look out for the poor child."

"*I'm* looking out for her!"

"I can look out for myself," Diana began, tired of being treated as if she wasn't able to speak for herself, when the front door suddenly flew open and Sophie burst onto the scene.

"Will someone kindly explain why the four of you saw fit to abandon me to a bunch of yokels whose idea of entertainment is to see who can spit the farthest?" she inquired indignantly.

"Diana wasn't well, and had to leave," Anton said.

"Oh, well, that explains everything!" she sneered. "What's the matter, Diana? Nothing as fatal as a hangnail, I hope?"

Weary of the whole conversation, Diana retorted, "No, Sophie. Sorry to disappoint you, but I think I'm going to survive."

"And you'll do it much faster without us hovering over you," Hortense decided. "Come along, Josette, and you, too, Sophie. We're not needed here. Diana's in good hands with Anton."

But Sophie, noticing that Anton had slipped his arm around Diana's waist, eyed them suspiciously. "There's something else going on here, if you ask me. Just what are the two of you up to?"

"Whatever it is," Anton informed her coldly, "it's our business, not yours."

"Not for long," Diana muttered, as the women went their separate ways. "At this rate, they'll soon be putting two and two together and coming up with four."

"With three, at any rate," he agreed. "Which is all the more reason we waste no time taking control of the situation."

"Taking control," she discovered, meant Anton calling in favors and securing an appointment with the best obstetrician in Aix, for ten o'clock on the Monday morning. The irony was not lost on Diana. Like mother, like daughter, she thought, the difference being that unlike Jeanne, she was not alone and desperate. At the very worst, she could afford to keep her baby and give it a good life.

And at the best? She slid a quick glance at Anton as the specialist joined them in the consulting room after examining her. Was he really as composed as he appeared?

The doctor didn't even bother to open the patient chart lying on his desk. "Congratulations, both of you. Today's advanced technology means we're able to confirm pregnancy much earlier than was once the case, and after running the necessary tests, I can say with certainty that you have a baby on the way."

Diana wilted in her seat, not sure whether to laugh or cry, but Anton leaned forward, focused, intense. "What about the nausea she's experiencing?"

"Perfectly normal, Monsieur de Valois. Desirable, even, since it indicates successful implantation of the embryo. Madame is in excellent health and I anticipate a healthy, full-term baby."

Anton heaved a great sigh, smiled and gripped her hand tightly in his. "And the due date?"

The specialist spared the patient chart a quick glance. "March 17, give or take a week."

"What about special instructions—level of activity, diet, that sort of thing?"

"Pregnancy is not an illness, *monsieur,*" the doctor said, smiling. "It's a natural condition caused by—"

"Trust me, Doctor," Anton interrupted, "I know what caused it. Now I'd like to be sure I do nothing to jeopardize it."

"No doubt!" The doctor permitted himself another small smile. "Harmony, lack of stress, support—these you can provide. For the expectant mother, at this stage my only recommendations are prenatal vitamins, a healthy diet, plenty of rest and regular exercise. Beyond that, she's free to lead a perfectly normal life as her energy allows."

"And you'll see her again when?"

"In one month, barring any unforeseen complications." He rose, dismissing them. "Relax, *monsieur.* You have nothing to worry about. Your lady is in fine shape. Good day, and remember to book an appointment with my receptionist before you leave."

As he escorted her across the street from the obstetrician's office to where he'd left the car—not the Range Rover she'd expected, but a sleek BMW he handled with the same sure expertise he brought to everything he did, Anton made no reference to the news they'd received. Instead he said quietly, "You had nothing but tea and toast at breakfast, and must be hungry. We'll have lunch somewhere on the Cours Mirabeau."

Diana nodded absently, staring unseeingly out of the window during the short drive there, lost in her own thoughts. Had her mother been overwhelmed by the bustle of activity, when she came here, alone and pregnant? Did she find it too much, after the slow pace of life in her native village? Was she afraid? Lonely? Or just glad to have escaped the probing scrutiny of all eyes, every time she set foot outside the house?

Anton parked the car in a square close to the Cours Mirabeau, a beautiful avenue lined with sidewalk cafés and bookshops, and alive with the sound of water. Large and small, simple and ornate, fountains splashed and bubbled and shot in clear green jets at every turn, casting shifting shadows over the facades of the buildings and lending texture to the deep shade of the plane trees.

"This will do," he decided, shepherding her into *Le Grillon,* an elegant terrace restaurant where a waiter showed them to a quiet corner table for two.

She ordered sole, lightly poached and mineral water with lime. Anton chose smoked salmon and spinach baked in a flaky pastry crust, and a glass of white wine which he sipped meditatively while they waited for their meal to arrive.

It was early yet, not quite noon, and there were few other patrons ordering lunch, which made his silence that much more oppressive. She thought he must be in shock; that even though she'd told him she was pretty sure she knew what the doctor's verdict would be, he hadn't really believed her.

Finally she could stand it no longer and, clearing her throat, spoke her mind. "You've been very quiet since we left the doctor's office, Anton, but sooner or later, we're going to have to talk about the elephant we're both pretending isn't sharing this table with us."

"The pregnancy, you mean?"

"What else!"

He responded by taking another mouthful of wine.

Did he think getting potted was going to change anything? "Look," she said, trying not to sound desperate, "I can see that you're shocked, but—"

"I'm not shocked at all," he cut in calmly. "I'm figuring things out and thinking how lucky we are that we have at least a little time on our side."

"Time?" she repeated, unsure where this was leading. "Time for what?"

"To plan our future and let people get used to the idea that we're a couple."

Confused, she stared at him. "What on earth are you talking about?"

"I'd have thought it was obvious," he said, lifting his clear gray gaze to her face. "If you're having my baby, Diana, we're getting married. As soon as possible and most definitely before summer's end. And don't even think about opposing me on this, because the matter is *not* up for discussion."

CHAPTER NINE

"YOU can't possibly be serious!" she stammered, when she finally found her voice. "We already agreed, when we first discussed it, that in the event I should be pregnant, marriage wasn't an option."

"No. We agreed not to jump to any premature conclusions until we knew for sure if you had conceived. Now that it's been confirmed that you have, marriage is the logical next step."

"In your antiquated world, maybe," she said, rendered almost speechless with indignation at his cold-blooded assessment of the situation, "but not in mine."

"You're carrying my baby, Diana," he reminded her loftily.

As if she was likely to forget! "That doesn't make me your chattel."

"That word again?" He laughed scornfully, as if such an outdated concept was beyond his understanding. "Stop over-reacting! I'm merely stating the obvious, which is that a man honors his obligation to take care of his own, and I can't think of a better way to do that than by making you my wife."

"Absolutely not," she said, firmly shutting out the insidious little voice whispering inside her head that she shouldn't be so quick to turn him down. Hadn't she dreamed about him almost every night for a month or more? Woken to find her body throbbing with hunger for him? Didn't she melt when she remembered his kisses, his touch?

"Why not? Does the prospect of taking me for your husband fill you with such distaste?"

"It's not that," she mumbled, refusing to meet his gaze.

"Then what's the problem?"

How could he be so blind? So obtuse? "*We* are!" she said emphatically. "For heaven's sake, we're strangers in all the ways that matter, and I'm not talking about something as trivial as not knowing each other's favorite foods or colors. Culturally and socially, we're poles apart. You're an aristocrat, and I'm…" *The illegitimate child of your housekeeper!*

Beset by the truth as she saw it, she wilted with despair. "I'm a commoner. An American, with no more understanding of what your heritage means to you, than you have of what baseball and hot dogs mean to people like me. Face it, Anton. With such barriers separating us, how can we even contemplate marriage, and expect it to work?"

Completely unfazed by her emotional outburst, he said calmly, "The only barriers are those you've erected in your mind. I've seen how smoothly you've adapted to a way of life different from what you're used to. I've seen how readily my aunts have accepted you—and trust me, Diana, they do not confer their approval lightly. You handle mobs of tourists with grace and intelligence. Treat people with respect and kindness. Quite frankly, these qualities alone are enough to convince me you're exactly the right woman to become my wife."

He lowered his voice to the seductive softness of midnight velvet. "But there's also my personal, very private experience, the memory of which still stirs me to desire. We made love only once, but it was enough for me to recognize a passion in your soul equal to that in mine. Together we were magnificent, and that alone is more than many couples ever achieve."

"Be reasonable!" she implored, even as that traitorous little voice urged her to forget reason and follow her heart. "I know nothing about your work, your ambitions—"

"That's where time is on our side. You can learn. Before our child is born, you will be as familiar with his inheritance as you are with your own name."

He was entangling her in a web of logic; hypnotizing her with his fatal magnetism. In a last desperate bid to escape, she said, "You seem to have forgotten that I have a job to do."

"Nonsense!" he scoffed, sweeping aside such a feeble excuse with the contempt it no doubt deserved. "To begin with, how do you expect to conduct tours when you're nauseated all the time? And even if that wasn't a problem, do you seriously think that I will allow my future wife to work for her keep? No, Diana. Until I find someone else to fill the position, my assistant manager will take over the job. As of this minute, your health, your well-being, come before all else."

Armed with such confidence, he could have turned the tide, had he wished. Stopped the clock and spun time backward, if it had pleased him to do so. Instead he made her the focus of his unswerving determination, and the resolve she fought so hard to preserve collapsed into a faint, bewildered, "Do you really think we can make it work?"

He folded her hand in his. Mesmerized her with his unblinking gaze. "I don't *think* we can, Diana. I *know* it."

Why was she opposing him? What were the alternatives if she persisted in refusing him? To give their child a life with only one parent, when he or she could easily have both? Anton would never allow it. To subject their child to a split existence and torn loyalties: summer with father and great-aunts; winter with mother? She herself wouldn't allow that.

To agree to his terms, and inherit the best of all worlds: a family of her own, not just with Anton and his aunts, but with her mother—and the hope that, one day, her connection to Jeanne would be a secret no longer? What greater gift could she offer, than to give Jeanne the chance to enjoy with her grandchild all the things she was denied with her own baby?

"Are you absolutely sure, Anton?"

"I am absolutely sure, Diana, believe me."

Oh, she wanted to! With all her heart, she wanted to fall in with his plans, and let her reservations evaporate in the heat of his conviction. But not once since their night together had he approached her as a man toward his lover. Not once had he tried to kiss her or be alone with her. Only now, when he knew for certain that she carried his child, did he profess to care.

On the other hand, how could she not believe him? His beautiful eyes couldn't lie. There was nowhere in their clear gray depths for the truth to hide.

"All right, then."

"You'll do it? You'll marry me?"

A tremor of nervous anticipation quivered through her heart. "I will."

"You won't regret this decision," he said. "Together, we'll be invincible, you'll see."

Diana hadn't expected their absence would go unnoticed, nor did it. They arrived back at the château with barely enough time to change before dinner, mostly because Anton, overriding her objections, insisted on spending the afternoon shopping for an engagement ring and having it sized to fit.

"Nice of you to ask if I felt like a jaunt into town." The last to come down for the cocktail hour, Sophie sidled up to him, all pouty lips and bedroom eyes. "I was bored silly, here by myself all day. What was so urgent that you had to race off without a word to anyone?"

"You'd have been even more bored if you'd come with us, Sophie," he replied smoothly. "Diana and I had business to attend to in Aix that concerned just the two of us."

"Oh, really?" Josette looked up eagerly and nudged Hortense. "Are you going to let us in on it?"

"Certainly." He came to where Diana sat sipping sparkling

water and furtively keeping her left hand hidden in the folds of her cocktail gown. "It's too soon for this," she'd protested, when he'd slipped the diamond solitaire on her finger. "We've known each other less than a month. No one's going to believe we're engaged."

"Then we'll have to convince them they're wrong, won't we?" he'd said, with his usual imperturbable certainty that he had the world by the tail.

Taking her hand now, he pulled her up to stand next to him and slipped his arm around her waist. "You're looking at a very happy man, *mesdames*. This afternoon, I asked Diana to marry me and I'm both honored and pleased to tell you that she accepted my proposal."

Given the aunts' uninhibited exclamations of delight and exuberant hugs, Sophie's reaction to the news might have passed undetected by the others, but Diana saw the color leach from her face and the sudden narrowing of her eyes.

Oblivious to any undercurrents, Hortense raised her glass. "We must have a toast! To you, my dear, dear nephew, and to your beautiful—!"

"This is a joke!" Sophie cut in, with a laugh so harsh, it ripped through the atmosphere like a saw. "Anton's pulling your leg. Tell her, Anton!"

Spearing his cousin with a quelling glare, Anton lifted Diana's left hand to reveal the diamond flashing blue fire in the light from the crystal wall sconces. "Does this look like a joke to you, Sophie?"

Her jaw dropped briefly. Then, with a superhuman effort, she wrestled herself under control. "No, it doesn't," she managed, pasting a grim smile on her face. "But am I the only one who finds this...*engagement* very sudden?"

"It's not sudden at all, as you'd know if you paid attention to anyone but yourself," Josette snapped. "Hortense and I guessed days ago that something like this was in the offing, and we couldn't be more delighted. When is the wedding to be, *mes chers enfants?*"

Anton bathed Diana in a victorious smile. "No later than the end of August, and sooner if I have any say in the matter. I want to take my wife away on our honeymoon before the grape harvest begins."

"That doesn't allow much time to make arrangements."

"Diana and I have discussed it, and decided on a small, discreet affair, *ma tante,*" he said. "Just family and a few close friends. It is, after all, a second marriage for both of us."

Sophie fixed Diana in a gimlet-eyed stare. "How many of your family will be attending?"

"None," Diana said.

"Why not?"

"I believe I already told you that my parents are dead and I was an only child."

"But you must have other relatives?"

"Not as far as I know," she said, the cost of having to deny her mother blinding her to just how much she'd revealed with her answer.

But Sophie leaped on it with avid hunger of a starving woman suddenly presented with a ten-course feast. "What kind of person doesn't *know* if she has relatives? Were you a foundling, or something?"

Broken only by a muffled gasp of outrage from one of the aunts, a drop of silence fell into the room and, like the ripples from a stone cast carelessly onto the calm surface of a pond, spread until Diana felt herself smothering in it. *So here it comes,* she thought, flinging an anguished glance at Anton. *The moment of truth, and the price one pays for keeping it hidden.*

Lifting her chin, she looked her enemy straight in the eye. "I was adopted at birth, if that's what you mean."

Sophie opened her eyes very wide, and shaped her lip-sticked mouth into a silent and protracted *Oh!* At length, she breathed "I see! No wonder you're so anxious to join this family, then."

"Sophie," Anton interposed, his voice coated with steely displeasure, "you're testing my patience sorely. Please stop. And if that's asking too much, then perhaps it's time you went back to Paris."

"And miss the wedding of the year?" She shot Diana a malicious smile. "I wouldn't dream of it!"

Dinner was a nightmare. Although Anton and the aunts made a valiant effort to behave as if nothing untoward had occurred, Diana felt their covert glances. Sick as much from emotional stress as pregnancy, she forced down most of the chestnut-flavored pumpkin soup which started the meal, but her stomach rebelled at the main course, a small guinea hen stuffed with foie gras, and bathed in mushroom sauce.

Of course, Sophie noticed, just as she noticed that Diana refused wine with the meal, and frequently dabbed at the little beads of perspiration dotting her upper lip. And being Sophie, she commented, cloaking her nasty little remarks in a veneer of concern as transparent as glass.

Finally Anton put an end to it. "Be silent, woman!" he exploded, rising from his chair so violently that he knocked over his wineglass and sent a stain red as blood soaking into the fine damask tablecloth. "We've all heard enough from you for one night!"

Then, without so much as a glance at Diana, he threw down his napkin and strode from the room.

The aunts stared at Sophie as if she was something they'd had to scrape off the bottom of their shoes. "Don't look at me like that," she snapped.

"We'd greatly prefer not to have to look at you at all," Hortense replied severely. "You're an offense to civilized society, Sophie Beauvais, and I thank God you're no relation of mine."

At that, Sophie, too, slammed out of her chair, though not with the same dramatic effect Anton had managed. "Like it or not, Hortense, I am a member of this family, and I refuse to sit here and be spoken to as if I were nothing but a glorified employee like someone else at this table."

Hortense lazily swirled the wine in her glass. "Then do us all a favor and leave."

Sophie did. In high dudgeon, and with a last malevolent glare at Diana.

"We're going to have to watch that one," Josette murmured, as the door banged closed. "Left to her own devices, she's capable of causing no end of trouble, and I'm afraid she has you in her sights, Diana."

"She thinks I'm not good enough for Anton, and she's probably right." *Because my falling in love with him doesn't change the fact that I'm here under false pretenses.*

Hortense patted her hand bracingly. "If, by that, you're referring to the circumstances concerning your birth, there's no shame attached to being adopted."

"Of course there isn't!" Josette crowded her on her other side and gave her a warm hug. "You do Anton an injustice to think he cares about that."

They were so kind, so willing to believe in her, that to her chagrin, Diana burst into tears. "I'm sorry," she wept. "I don't know what's wrong with me. I don't usually cry at the drop of a hat, but Anton was so furious—"

"Not with you, *ma chère,*" Hortense pointed out. "This was a very special day for the two of you, and that witch of a cousin is the one who spoiled it. You'd both be less than human if you weren't affected by such uncalled-for spite."

"Hortense is right," Josette said gently. "You worry about important things, such as choosing a wedding dress, and leave Sophie Beauvais to us. We'll make sure she doesn't cause any further trouble."

They meant well, but Diana had seen the hostility in Sophie's eyes and knew it would take more than these two well-meaning women to put an end to her machinations. She'd earmarked Anton for herself, and if she couldn't have him, she'd stop at nothing to make sure no one else did.

And if, in the process, she ruined a few lives? Diana could well imagine her answer. *That's what happens in war. There are bound to be casualties.*

But Diana herself was the one most at fault. If she'd been honest with Anton from the start, Sophie might still be full of resentment toward someone she considered an interloper, but she'd be powerless to make innocent bystanders the target of her rage.

Too ashamed to sit there a moment longer, the undeserving recipient of the aunts' generous outpouring of sympathy, Diana begged to be excused. She had to find Anton. The time had come to tell him everything.

She'd no sooner left the room and started down the hall than she ran into Jeanne. "I was just coming to get you," her mother said. "You have a phone call. It came through to the central switchboard, as all calls do after nine o'clock in the evening, but I'll transfer it to the west wing library, where you'll have privacy." Then, her eyes full of concern, she added, "You appear very upset, Diana. Is there anything I can do?"

Oh, if only she could pour out her heart to this kind and gentle soul! If only she dared say, *I think I'm your daughter, and I need so badly for you to be my mother because, in trying to find you, I've made such a mess of things and I don't have anyone to turn to for advice.*

But even if she had the right to unburden herself to Jeanne, now was not the time. Not until she'd spoken to Anton. So, "No, thank you, Jeanne," she choked. "It's just been a very long day, that's all, and I'm very tired."

"Then while you take your call, I'll fix you a cup of herbal tea to help you sleep, and bring it to your room."

Puzzled as to who'd be phoning her at this hour, Diana shut herself in the library, a large, dimly lit room she'd visited only once before. Bookshelves lined the walls. A brass table holding cognac and a selection of liqueurs stood to one side of a big stone fireplace. Flanking the hearth were four comfortable, high-backed leather reading chairs with side tables, on one of which was an empty brandy snifter. But these details she noticed only peripherally as she crossed to where the phone sat on a desk at the far end of the room.

Lifting the handset, she waited until she heard the click of the call being connected, before uttering a guarded, "Hello? This is Diana Reeves."

Carol's voice blasted across the miles. "Finally! I've been trying to get through to you for the last two hours."

"Sorry," she said. "I've had my cell phone turned off all day."

"No kidding, Sherlock! Why else do you think I jumped through hoops to get the château listing from the international directory? For crying out loud, Diana, you said you'd let me know what the doctor said. I walked the floor half the night, frantic with worry when I didn't hear from you—much to my husband's annoyance, I might add!"

"I forgot," she said contritely. "I'm really sorry, Carol, but so much happened today that it slipped my mind completely."

"Well?" Carol's impatience hummed over the line. "Now that I've tracked you down, don't keep me hanging. What's the verdict?"

"I'm pregnant all right."

Her voice softened. "Ah, Diana, I was hoping for a different answer. Does Anton know?"

"Yes. He was there when the obstetrician gave us the news."

"How did he take it?"

"He wants to marry me," she said bleakly. "He even bought me an engagement ring."

"Did you accept it?"

She looked down at the diamond solitaire adorning her finger. "I suppose so. I'm wearing it."

"And you sound about as thrilled as if he'd asked you to get all your teeth pulled. What's the problem?"

"Oh, Carol, that you even have to ask! You know very well what the problem is."

"If I did, I wouldn't have put the question to you, so spit it out. Are you saying you don't care for him as much as you thought you did?"

"Hardly! I once read that when it comes to falling in love, ten minutes is all it takes, but I never believed it until I met him. He's everything I ever hoped to find in a man."

"How does he feel about you?"

"He acts as if he cares. He says he does."

"Then, I repeat—what's the problem?"

"His cousin, Sophie. She's still here, and sniffing around looking for trouble."

"So let her look. It's not as if you've done anything wrong."

"Yes, I have. It's wrong to agree to marry a man, and not tell him everything he has a right to know."

"What are you getting at?" Carol asked sharply.

"I have to come clean with him. I have to tell him what brought me here in the first place. I can't risk having his mean-spirited cousin stumble on the truth and blindside him with it. He deserves to hear it from me."

"You're forgetting one thing, Diana," Carol reminded her soberly. "This isn't your secret to tell. It's Jeanne's—if she is, indeed, your mother. And she might not want it spread abroad. At the very least, you have to speak to her first, and only if she agrees, do you have the right to mention it to Anton."

Much though she'd have liked to argue the point, Diana had to acknowledge her friend was right. "I know," she said. "At bottom, I've known it all along. Thanks for the straight talk, Carol."

"Hey, what else are friends for?" she said. "Listen, you sound beat, so I'll hang up now, but keep me posted, okay?"

"I will. Love to you and Annie, and my apologies to Tim."

She replaced the handset and stood a moment, slumped against the edge of the desk. She'd do what she had to do, but not tonight. She didn't have the energy.

Rubbing her temples wearily, she turned to leave the room and let out a strangled gasp of horror as a reading lamp flicked on at the other end of the room, to reveal Sophie curled up in the big leather chair beside the fireplace.

"I haven't figured out what your big, dark secret is, and I really don't care," she said conversationally, "but I can tell you this—whatever you think you know, there's a whole lot more you *don't* know. And if you've convinced yourself that Anton's marrying you because he gives a damn about you, you're delusional, and I can prove it."

CHAPTER TEN

DON'T listen.... This woman is not to be trusted.... She's a negative, embittered force bent on destroying you because she believes you've come between her and Anton.... Walk away before she succeeds.... Walk away now...!

The words hammered at Diana, appealing to her common sense, her self-respect, her belief in her fiancé, and every other instinct geared toward her own survival and preservation of the status quo. But her body refused to obey. Try though she might to propel herself toward the door, her feet sank into a morass of uncertainty provoked by Sophie's amusement and the utter conviction in her tone.

Recognizing her dilemma, Sophie unfolded her long legs from the chair, wove her way to the liquor table and poured a hefty two inches of cognac into the empty brandy snifter now cradled between her fingers. "So Anton's knocked you up," she drawled insolently. "I was wondering why you weren't swilling back the champagne to celebrate your sudden engagement—which, by the way, suddenly makes *oh*-so-much sense."

"How much have you had to drink, Sophie?"

She sauntered over to where Diana stood with the desk at her back. "Not nearly enough to prevent me from figuring you're about as gullible as a chicken trying to stare down a fox, *petite imbecile!*" she replied gleefully.

Diana couldn't remember seeing her smile quite so broadly before, and wished she hadn't bothered now. It was not a pleasant sight. "Get out of my way, Sophie. I've got better things to do than stand here listening to your drunken ramblings."

"Well, of course, little mother!" she cooed. But instead she stepped closer, enough to infuse the air with the overpowering scent of her perfume. "Just satisfy my curiosity on one point, before you go. Has Anton told you how his first wife died?"

She endowed the question with such ungodly delight that a quiver of dread prickled over Diana. Trying hard to dismiss it, she said flatly, "No. And I wasn't insensitive enough to ask. I assumed she'd died of some terminal illness, or else been killed in an accident."

"Why assume? Why not simply ask?"

"I didn't feel it was my place to probe into something I know must have caused him great pain. What matters is that it's in the past. Anton's over it."

"You think?" Sophie let out a squawk of scornful laughter. "You'd better deliver a healthy son, or you'll find out fast enough just how 'over' it he is! Oh, Diana, you poor, foolish creature! You have no idea of what's really going on. No idea, at all!"

How long are you going to let this woman taunt you like this? Diana's pride demanded. *If you can't bring yourself to walk away, then call her bluff, and have done with, but don't give her the satisfaction of knowing she has you twisting in the wind.*

Ashamed, she grabbed her dwindling gumption and forced it to assert itself. "Spare me more riddles, Sophie," she said curtly. "Either say what's on your mind, or save your breath."

"Well…if you insist." Sophie ran the tip of her tongue over her lips as if she were about to sample a deliciously forbidden morsel. "But you might want to sit down to hear this."

"I'll stand, thanks."

She shrugged. "Suit yourself," she crooned, and took another sip of brandy.

"I'm losing patience, Sophie. Let's hear it."

"Well...all right...I'll tell you—because really, you have the right to know." She made a big production of staring at the ceiling, her forefinger pressed melodramatically to her chin. "Let's see now, how do I begin? I guess, since it has all the trappings of a fairy tale, at least at the start, there's only one way.

"Once upon a time, a gently reared young French woman called Marie-Louise fell in love with, and married a handsome French Count named Anton. It was quite the ideal match, you understand, both of them being of aristocratic birth. For a while—several years, in fact—theirs was a match apparently made in heaven. But, as with most fairy tales, there had to be a wicked something or other to spoil the couple's bliss, except, in this case, it wasn't a stepmother, or a witch, it was a fatal flaw within the bride herself."

How Sophie was enjoying this, Diana realized, sickened by the relish with which the woman wallowed in her tale. Yet she continued to listen anyway, a captive audience to a story whose shades of tragedy grew darker with every word.

"In the end, it became more than the poor creature could bear. Oops!" Sophie stopped and let loose with another cackle of unholy mirth. "Unfortunate choice of words, that! Let me rephrase it. Unable to face the disappointment in her husband's eyes, or the travesty her marriage had become, the unhappy wife threw herself off the roof of the château one morning. One of the gardeners found her body on the terrace."

"Oh, God!" Recoiling in cold horror, Diana pressed both hands to her mouth.

"She made quite a mess, let me tell you. Of course, the police became involved, which by itself was bad enough because never a breath of scandal had ever touched the de Valois name before, but imagine, if you can, how much worse it became when suspicion arose that perhaps she had not committed suicide at all, but had been murdered. By her husband."

"You're lying!" Diana cried, her heart fluttering madly in her throat.

"Well, I admit he was eventually cleared. The faithful came forward in droves to provide proof he was nowhere near the château when the incident occurred. But rest assured that he drove her to her death, and has her blood on his hands as surely as if he'd pushed her off that parapet. And why, you ask? Because she couldn't give him an heir, though, God knows, it wasn't for lack of trying."

"I don't believe you! You're making this up because Anton wants me, not you."

"Don't believe me, then," Sophie said calmly. "But ask yourself this. When did he suddenly become so enamored of you that he wanted you for his wife—before he found out you were pregnant—or after? More to the point, has he ever actually come out and said those three magic little words, *I love you?*"

The questions flew like missiles, scoring a direct hit where Diana was most vulnerable. In response, the doubts she'd tried so hard to subdue rose up in protest again, crying out to be heard.

Why, if he found her so desirable, had he never attempted to come back to her bed? Never stolen a kiss in the hall, or nudged her knee with his under the table at dinner, or reassured her with a loving touch, a whispered endearment? Why, as he'd slipped his ring on her finger, had he kissed her with lips as devoid of warmth as the mistral in January?

Dear heaven, was it possible that his urgent insistence on their marrying owed nothing to his unimpeachable sense of honor, and everything to expedience? If Sophie was to be believed, the answer seemed plain enough.

And to think she'd felt guilty about not telling him she was adopted! Numb with shock, Diana sagged against the desk.

"Just as I suspected!" her tormentor crowed, accurately inter-preting the dismay she couldn't hide. "Face it, Diana, you're merely a convenient brood mare. As long as you're carrying his child, he'll cosset you and lead you to believe he has only your best interests at heart, but once you've produced the requisite heir, you'll have served your purpose. So forget any ideas you have of assuming the role of chatelaine, or of being a part of your baby's life. You'll become redundant as soon as the brat's weaned."

Like hell she would! Harvey had denied her a child, and she'd be damned if she'd let another man rob her, too. "You forget, Sophie, that I'm the mother of this child, and no one is going to deprive me of my rights—always assuming, of course, that this story you've spun for me tonight is the truth."

"You think I made it up?"

"I think you're capable of such a stunt, yes."

Sophie shook her head pityingly. "Then get Anton to show you the upper floor of the east wing—oh, but I forgot. He keeps it locked all the time, doesn't he, and refuses to discuss the reason for it? Aren't you the least bit curious as to why?"

"I know why. It's to cut down on maintenance. Jeanne told me so."

Another hoot of merriment split the air. "Jeanne would swear the earth is flat, if Anton instructed her to say so. But don't take my word for it. Do yourself a favor, get hold of that key, and go see for yourself what's hidden behind that locked door." She drained her brandy snifter and set it down on the desk. "And then, if you've any sense at all, you'll hotfoot it back to America before you find yourself legally bound to Anton in marriage…and long before your child is born!"

He paced the terrace, unease sitting in the pit of his stomach like badly digested food. Not that he cared that Diana had been adopted, or that she'd not seen fit to mention it to him sooner. After all, they both carried a lot of history yet to be revealed. But her guilty reaction to what was, on the surface, an innocent enough admission, her hunted inability to meet his gaze, the way her face had drained of color, brought back with vivid clarity the events of that night at the inn—how long ago it now seemed!—when they'd met.

His first and most abiding impression, that she wasn't all she pretended to be and couldn't be trusted, had been confirmed by the telephone conversation he'd overheard outside her room. Yet somewhere between then and now, he'd pushed to the back of his mind that the reason he'd brought her into his household was to monitor the possible enemy in their midst and, if necessary, neutralize her actions. Instead he'd lowered his guard enough to let her insinuate herself into his arms and his heart.

Damn her anyway, with her big, innocent blue eyes and sweet vulnerable mouth! Damn her gentle charm, her spirit and fire, her soft, womanly curves, and everything else about her that made him forget to be careful! That made him, even now, hot and hard and aching for her!

Increasingly restless, he spun on his heel and paced the length of the terrace again. Where the devil was she? Dinner had to be over, by now. Why hadn't she come looking for him, to chase away his doubts with a smile, a touch, a straightforward explanation? He was willing to listen, even willing to understand if, having deceived him in the beginning, she'd now had a change of heart. People made mistakes—he certainly had!—but acknowledging them, trying to put them right, made them forgivable. Most of the time, at least.

But not always. Not with Marie-Louise. She'd made certain of that. Good God, was he about to take another wife who refused to trust him enough to confide her deepest fears, her most closely guarded secrets?

Turning again, he glanced up and saw that the light had come on in Diana's room, the one place he'd avoided, except for the night she'd conceived, because he hadn't been willing to risk compromising her reputation in his household. Well, reputation be damned! There was more at stake here than his misplaced sense of honor.

* * *

She had no idea she wasn't alone in the suite until, having changed into a short cotton nightgown and washed her face, she came back to her little sitting room and picked up the cup of herbal tea Jeanne had left on the low table in front of the love seat. Even then, she didn't notice him right away. Not until his shadow, elongated and sinister, reached across the floor to block the light from the lamp on the *escritoire*.

The tea splashed down the front of her nightgown, then, stinging where it touched her skin. "Good *grief,* Anton, you scared me!" she uttered, on a choking cry.

"Did I?" he said softly.

No word of apology, she noticed. No expression of concern that such a sudden shock might jeopardize her pregnancy. Nothing at all, in fact, but an icy, unnatural calm.

She had a pretty good idea what prompted it. He was hurt and angry that she hadn't told him about her adoption—maybe even alarmed because her being unable to supply any medical history of her biological parents could possibly pose a threat to the health of her unborn child. "I suppose," she murmured, "you're here because of what came out at dinner tonight, about my being adopted."

He rocked back on his heels. "You suppose right. Why didn't you tell me sooner, Diana?"

He was giving her the opening to confess everything, and an hour ago, she'd have seized it with both hands. But that was before her mind had been poisoned with ugly suspicions. Much though she wished it was otherwise, there'd been a ring of truth to Sophie's revelations that couldn't be dismissed. Suddenly everything to do with Anton was suspect, and until her doubts could be put to rest, Diana was determined to keep her secrets to herself.

No longer trembling with fright, she set the cup back on its saucer, took the small linen napkin from the tray and mopped at the stains on her nightgown. "It didn't occur to me. It's not something I dwell on, any more than I do that I'm five feet six, and a natural blonde. It's part of who I am, that's all." She glanced up and met his gaze unflinchingly. "But it seems to disturb *you*, Anton. Why is that? Does it make me less worthy in your eyes?"

Outrage sparked in his eyes. "I'm insulted you'd even ask such a question, Diana! What kind of man do you take me for?"

"I'm not sure," she said. "Perhaps the kind who values lineage, more than most. You are, after all, *le Comte de Valois,* and I'm probably illegitimate. In other words, a bastard, in the true sense of the word."

"Unlike me, you mean, who's a prime example of the corrupted version of the word, and acts like a perfect fool on occasion?"

"I didn't say that."

"But you thought it." His mouth curled in faint amusement. "Come on, Diana," he challenged. "Admit it."

I'm admitting nothing! she determined, steeling herself against his insidious charm. Apart from anything else, the nausea that had been building for the last hour was suddenly imminent, leaving her in no shape to prolong the discussion, even if she'd wanted to. "It's been a very long day, and I'd like to go to bed—get some sleep, I mean. Can we please continue this another time?"

She'd have done better to say nothing. Closing the distance between them, he tilted up her chin, the better to examine her face. "You're feeling sick again, aren't you?"

"No," she said, closing her eyes against his probing stare, and willing her dinner to stay put long enough for her to get rid of him. Throwing up in front of him was more than she could handle; the ultimate indignity in an evening beset by one affront after another. "I just need to lie down."

"You need to change your nightgown, first." He plucked the damp garment away from her body. "Did you burn yourself with the tea?"

"No. I'm fine." She swatted feebly at his hands. "Please just go, Anton, and…"

It was no good. She couldn't keep up the pretense. Consigning dignity to hell, she lurched away from him, staggered from the sitting room, through the bedroom, and made it to the bathroom in the nick of time. Dropping to her knees, she hung her head over the toilet bowl and let go, too immersed in misery to care that he'd followed her, or that his hand smoothed the hair away from her face.

"Oh, that was fun," she panted, collapsing against the side of the bathtub when the retching finally subsided. "How long did the doctor say it would last?"

He took a washcloth from the stack piled on the vanity, rinsed it in cold water and knelt before her to wipe her face. "Usually just for the first three months, and you're already halfway there. Another six weeks, and you'll be through it."

She shuddered. "This is all your fault!"

"I daresay you're right, and I'm sorry…for everything. I had no business coming here and bullying you."

"It doesn't matter," she said wearily. "It's over now."

"It might be over, but it matters a very great deal. Your health and well-being are my responsibility, Diana, and the last thing I want is to distress you in any way. I'd never forgive myself if something happened to you or my baby."

My baby, he said. Not *her* baby, or at the very least, *their* baby.

As long as you're carrying his child, he'll cosset you and lead you to believe he has only your best interests at heart, but once you've produced the requisite heir, you'll have served your purpose….

Sophie's word floated back to haunt her, a cruel reminder of a past he seemed loath to mention. But for the knowledge that tipping her hand would give him the advantage she presently had, Diana would have challenged him to tell her how his first wife had died—and why.

"I'm perfectly fine now," she said, struggling to her feet and wanting only to be rid of him before temptation got the better of discretion. "You can leave with an easy mind."

"Not until you've changed this for a clean one, and I've seen you safely into bed," he told her, and to her horror, grabbed the hem of her nightgown and lifted it past her hips, and past her waist.

"Stop that!" she moaned, feebly trying to yank it down again.

Too little, and much too late! He'd already seen everything she had to show, and was staring at it with bemused fascination.

"Why, look at you!" he whispered.

"I'd just as soon not, and I'd definitely prefer that you don't," she spat.

He circled her nipple with a gentle fingertip, cupped the weight of her breast in the warm palm of his hand. "But you're beautiful, Diana. Beautiful in a different way from how you were before."

"No surprise there," she said, willing her traitorous flesh to ignore the seduction of his touch. "Pregnancy does that to a woman, so I'm told."

He brought his other hand to rest against her abdomen, splaying his fingers to encompass the width of her pelvis. "To think you carry a tiny life in here—my son or daughter…!" He lifted his gaze to hers, and she saw his eyes were bright with unshed tears. "It's a miracle. *You* are a miracle!"

Heat coiled within her. Left her nipples taut and aching. Left her wet and swollen at her core. Should he slide his hand lower, slip his finger between her thighs and the folds of her flesh, and touch her, she'd climax.

In outlining what she might expect in the coming months, the doctor had warned her this kind of thing could happen. "As for sex, it's been my experience that women either want no part of it, or they can't get enough of it," he'd advised her bluntly, as he drew blood from her arm. "Listen to your body. It will tell you what it needs."

It was telling her in no uncertain terms. Another second, and she'd be tearing at Anton's clothes, begging him to make love to her, there on the cool marble bathroom floor.

"Right now, I don't feel beautiful," she said shakily, "and the only miracle will be if I make it to bed without throwing up again. So if you must help, please look in the right of the top dresser drawer in my bedroom, and bring me the fresh nightgown you'll find there."

"Yes," he murmured, his gaze lingering one last time on her naked body, and drinking in the sight. "Certainly. Right away."

The second his back was turned, she grabbed the terry robe hanging on the bathroom door, thrust her arms into the sleeves, and secured the belt very firmly around her waist.

"I don't see any nightgowns in this drawer," she heard him say.

Of course he didn't. Moving swiftly to the bedroom, she joined him at the dresser and pulled open the next drawer down. "I just remembered, I put them in here," she said, with a convincing display of apology. "Sorry for the mix-up."

"That's okay, *ma chère*. No harm done."

Not much there wasn't! She tossed the gown on the bed and regarded him expectantly. "Yes…well, good night then."

She needed to get him out of her suite, out of her blood. Needed to sit calmly and consider her next move. To trust, or not to trust? To search for answers that would either condemn or exonerate him—or to dismiss everything Sophie had told her as the unfounded ravings of a woman driven to desperate lengths by jealousy?

"Just one more thing before I go, Diana." He tucked a strand of hair behind her ear, and dipped his head lower, bringing his face close to hers.

Don't let him kiss you! You'll be lost, if you do…!

Stepping quickly out of range, she faked a yawn behind her hand. "Oh, please, Anton! Can't it wait until morning?"

If he noticed how she shied away from him, he hid it well.

"That's just it," he said, his eyes mapping her face, feature by feature. "I'm leaving early in the morning for business meetings in Toulouse and won't be back until the day after tomorrow. I'd invite you come with me, but given the shape you're in—"

"Not a good idea. Not right now. But thank you for the thought." Her movements as jerky and uncoordinated as her speech, she scuttled to the little foyer and opened the door.

"You're welcome." He paused with his hand on the doorknob and searched her face again. "Take care of yourself while I'm gone. I'll miss you."

"I'll miss you, too," she lied.

His glance slid from her eyes to her mouth. Drifted lower, and lingered at the vee formed by the terry robe where it crossed over her breasts. "Will you?"

Her fist shot up and clutched the fabric tightly. Dear heaven, of all the times to grow a cleavage! "Of course."

A shadow crossed his face. "Diana, are we…okay?"

"What do you mean?"

"Is everything okay between us? Because if there's something not right, if you're troubled about something, you can talk to me, you know."

May God forgive her, she looked him straight in the eye and lied again. "Everything's fine."

He hesitated a moment longer, then lifted his shoulders in a faint shrug. "I guess that's it, then. See you in a couple of days."

"Yes," she said. "Drive safely."

"Will do." He dropped a dry, impersonal kiss on her cheek, and a moment later was gone.

She locked the door then, went to the bathroom, took off the terry-cloth robe and stared at herself in the full-length mirror. His voice all husky and deep, he'd looked at her and said, *You're beautiful in a different way.* To her critical eye, though, the only noticeable change was the tracery of blue veins on her breasts that left them looking a bit like a pair of bulbous road maps, marked in the middle with nipples gone from pale pink to dark rose. Hardly the kind of thing to inspire poets to wax lyrical, or artists to create masterpieces.

But if Sophie was to be believed, he hadn't been concerned with Diana's outward appearance. The place he'd found beauty was in her womb where his child lay.

And if Sophie had fabricated her story…?

Diana pulled on the clean nightgown, brushed her teeth and took a last look in the mirror, her mind made up. "All that stands between you and the answer is the key to the east wing," she told her image. "Fortunately you have all day tomorrow to find it."

CHAPTER ELEVEN

IT DIDN'T take all day, it took all of five minutes, although waiting for the right opportunity to get started seemed interminable. By half past ten, though, the aunts had left for their weekly shopping spree in Aix, and Sophie, seeming anxious to avoid contact with her at all costs, lay stretched out beside the swimming pool, slathered in tanning oil.

Deciding the two most logical places to look were Anton's office and his private apartment, Diana chose the latter first. Apart from the distant hum of a vacuum cleaner in the vicinity of the dining room, the house was quiet and the upstairs area deserted.

Like hers, his suite consisted of a small foyer, and two rooms, but where her sitting room was furnished in silks and delicate pastels, his was all burgundy leather, stark-white walls and rich, dark wood. A man's room, with a pedestal writing desk, small bar, television and stereo unit, and bookshelves.

Heart thumping, she went first to the desk, which had three deep drawers down either side, separated by a shallow center drawer above the knee-hole. Beginning with the center drawer, she carefully eased it open, and stared in stunned disbelief at what she saw. There, tossed in among a collection of pens and pencils in a divided tray, lay a large, ornate key she recognized immediately as the mate of the large, ornate lock on the east wing door.

"Why," she murmured to herself, "if he is so obsessed with

keeping people out of that part of the château, would he not keep this better hidden—inside a hollowed-out book, for instance, or behind a picture, in a wall safe?"

Her conscience promptly supplied the answer. *Because, Diana, he has no reason to think anyone in his loyal household would deliberately go against his wishes and force entry into an area he's deemed off-limits, or be sneaky enough to search his suite behind his back. And doesn't that leave you blushing with shame?*

Yes, it did—but not enough to stop her from slipping the key into the side pocket of her skirt. She might have thought twice about violating his trust if her sole intent had been to determine the wisdom of going ahead with the marriage. But this concerned the future of their child, and she'd go to whatever lengths she must to secure that.

The drive to Toulouse went well the next morning, despite his having had a lousy sleep. He was on the road by five, and with little traffic to contend with, arrived in plenty of time for his first appointment at ten. Yet for all that the meeting was of vital interest and importance to him, he found his mind frequently straying to Diana.

There'd been something "off" about her, last night. Even after they'd smoothed over their little contretemps, she'd remained distant, and so damned eager to be rid of him, she'd practically pushed him out the door. He wasn't a man prone to unwarranted anxiety, but as the morning dragged on, he couldn't shake off the vague sense that they'd reached a crisis point in their relationship.

A week ago, he'd have taken that as a sign to step back and weigh carefully the pros and cons of their relationship before taking it to the next level. Measured his pervasive doubts about her trustworthiness against his growing emotional attachment to her, and let the result dictate his next move. But that was before he'd seen her naked for the first time since they'd had sex. Before he'd found himself so deeply moved by the faint flush of pregnancy touching her body, that he'd wanted nothing more than to drop to his knees at her feet and adore her.

Until then, he'd have said, had he been asked, that he'd come to terms with her condition well enough. But he'd realized at that moment that he'd accepted it at a cerebral level only. Suddenly the emotional half of the equation hit home, and its impact had almost felled him.

This slender, delicate, beautiful woman would grow big with his child. Because of what he'd done, a few months from now she'd bleed and she'd sweat and she'd cry out with pain. And instead of punishing him for being the cause, she'd reward him with a son or daughter.

Where the hell did he get off, then, continuing to harbor doubts about her? To look for hidden motives? What did it matter that they'd started out on separate routes, with different ends in mind? The simple fact was, everything had changed not, as he'd once supposed, when they learned she was pregnant, but at the very moment of conception, when he'd lost himself in her silken heat, and she'd called out his name on a tremulous sigh of passion, and somehow taken hold of his heart and never given it back again.

Was this love—the kind that bound a man and woman together for life? He didn't know. Wasn't even sure he'd ever known. But of one thing he was certain. The time had come to let go of the suspicion. To stop wondering what she might try to take away from him, and focus instead on the hope and the joy and the promise she brought to his life.

"*Certainement,*" he concurred, realizing his colleagues were proposing to adjourn the meeting for lunch in the old part of the city. "Whatever you decide is fine with me."

But she stayed in his mind, and later, on his way back to his car after oysters at a café in the Vieux Quartier, a display of estate jewelry in an antique shop window caught his eye. Pushing open the door, he went inside the shop and cast around for something special to take home to her.

As a peace offering? A bribe?

No. As a symbol of a new beginning, and better times to come. Not diamonds, he decided. They were too cold, too hard, for her tender heart. Not the heavy gold necklace studded with five carat rubies, either. It was too massive for her slender neck.

"If price is not a factor, perhaps these might be what you're looking for," the wizened old man behind the counter said, taking a rope of pearls from a case behind him and laying it tenderly on a black velvet pad. "They are round South Sea pearls, between nine and nine-and-a-half millimeters, and as you see, *monsieur,* are perfectly matched. Because they are old, the body color, which is normally white, has a creamy overtone, but the luster is extraordinary because of the thickness of the nacre."

Heat curled low in Anton's belly. Both body color and luster, he thought, reminded him exactly of the bloom on Diana's skin. Warm, glowing, and utterly perfect. It would have given him the greatest pleasure to drape her from head to foot in a dozen such strings, had they been available.

"I'll take them," he said, the need to see her, to touch her urgent in his blood. But he had business to conduct first, and made it to his afternoon meeting with seconds to spare.

Tired from their trip, the aunts retired earlier than usual after dinner, and since Anton wasn't there to bait, Sophie saw no need to hang around, either. Even so, before taking a flashlight and creeping along the gallery to the east wing, Diana waited an extra half hour after the château sank into that deep silence indicative of a house at peace for the night.

The key turned smoothly in the lock. The heavy oak door swung open on oiled hinges. Leaving it slightly ajar so that she could make a fast escape if necessary, she passed through, and with the aid of her flashlight's beam, found the switch that turned on the sconces set in the walls of a long hall that was, in effect, an extension of the gallery itself.

She hadn't been sure what to expect as she came to the end of the corridor and opened a second door that led into a large, predominantly square room with a sitting nook set in the rounded section that followed the curve of the east tower. Dilapidation and decay, reminiscent of something out of a ghost story, perhaps, complete with the scurrying of tiny mice feet? But apart from a few cobwebs and a little dust, the handsomely furnished former master suite might have been occupied as recently as that morning. And *that* proved more horrifying than anything her imagination had been able to devise, as she realized when she ventured farther into forbidden territory and discovered twin en suite dressing rooms and bathrooms.

Those she presumed to have been Anton's had been stripped bare, but Marie-Louise's full-length formal gowns, cocktail dresses and chic daytime outfits still hung behind mirrored doors in her dressing room. Cashmere sweaters arranged by color lay neatly folded in glass-fronted drawers. Footwear for every conceivable occasion, from spindle-heeled, sequined evening shoes to riding boots, stood cheek by jowl on sloping shelves. Crystal perfume bottles and body lotions remained on the dressing table, as well as her chased silver hand mirror and hairbrush, the latter even with a few long, dark hairs caught in its bristles.

In the main room, a lace-trimmed peignoir had been tossed over the bed. A pair of satin mules lay in crooked disarray on the rug next to it, as if they'd been cast off in a hurry. A gold locket on a chain, and a plain gold wedding band had been abandoned at the base of a table lamp.

On top of a carved dresser were two photographs. The first, a wedding picture in a heavy silver frame, showed a younger, more carefree Anton smiling into the camera, and beside him, his dark-haired beauty of a bride. Sunlight glanced off the diamonds at her throat. A summer breeze tugged playfully at her gossamer-fine silk illusion veil. She looked happy, radiant, full of vitality; a young wife deeply in love with her husband.

But the second, a candid shot of Marie-Louise sitting alone in the gardens, told a different story. Here, the photographer had captured a woman whose spirit was locked in torment and whose body had grown thin and gaunt with sorrow. Although still beautiful, her dark eyes had lost their light, her mouth its laughter. Her skin was stretched taut over bones that looked too brittle to bear her weight. And why?

Scattered over the top of the bedside table, fertility charts, ovulation monitors and digital thermometers spelled out the yearning of a woman desperate to conceive. Sophie, it appeared, had told the truth on one score, at least.

Driven by growing dismay and morbid curiosity, Diana opened the mullioned door set to one side of the curved tower wall and, stepping out, found herself on a narrow walkway that ran parallel to the east-facing facade of the château. Above her, the mansard roof rose steeply toward the star-speckled sky. Below lay the quiet gardens and peaceful Provencal countryside, washed with moonlight and painted with shadows. And the only thing between her and them? A wall topped with broad coping stones, low enough that even a child could have scaled it.

As the likelihood hit home that Sophie had told the truth in every respect, and that Marie-Louise had indeed fallen to her death from there, a wave of nausea that had nothing to do with her pregnancy swept over Diana. With a broken cry, she sank to her knees and hugged her arms over her stomach.

It was almost midnight when he eased the BMW into the fore-court, and killed the engine. No point in waking up the entire household at that hour, especially not Diana who needed her sleep, he decided, keying the remote entry code to let himself inside the château. But the minute he stepped through the front door and went to rearm the security system, he saw at once that something was wrong. The signal light beside Zone 5 was flashing.

Someone was in the upper gallery, and whoever it was didn't know that, in addition to the building's perimeter alarms, unused sections of the house were protected every night by infrared security beams which, when broken, tripped their relays. Could be the kitchen cat had escaped and found her way up to the third floor, he rationalized, but he'd check it out anyway.

The gallery lay in darkness and it wasn't until he turned on the lights that he noticed the door to the east wing was open. He knew then not only that he couldn't blame the cat, but that whoever was trespassing in an area well-known to be off-limits, had also snooped through his private suite to find the key that would give her access.

And that he was dealing with a woman was as much a foregone conclusion, as her identity.

Fury boiling in his blood, he strode the length of the gallery, passed into the hall beyond and covered the remaining distance to the bedroom. "Damn you, Sophie!" he roared, slamming its door back on its hinges. "How dare you intrude in here, and what the devil are you after?"

Although at first glance the suite appeared deserted, a soft whimper of distress drew his attention to the open door leading to the walkway. At that, his rage died, chased away by a chilling sense of déjà vu. *Not again,* he prayed, his mind assailed by blood-soaked memories of a tragedy he should have foreseen and been able to prevent. *Dear God, not again!*

But his dread persisted. As surely as he knew Sophie had come to Provence a sad, embittered woman hoping for another shot at marriage with a man who could afford her, he also knew he was not, nor ever could be, that man. He'd thought she knew it, too

But if his announcing he planned to marry Diana had driven her over the edge of reason…if she'd decided she'd couldn't face being cast aside again by a man who didn't want her…?

Galvanized by fear, he raced to the open door, only to stumble to a halt on the threshold, his vision impaired by the sudden change from light to dark. "Sophie?" he called softly, peering blindly into the night. "Where are you?"

After a second or so, a figure rose from the shadow of the parapet, a pale blur in the gloom, too slight to be his cousin. "Here. And I'm not Sophie," Diana replied.

Supporting herself with one hand against the wall, she stumbled past him into the room, her face ashen, her expression frozen. Shocked almost speechless, he followed her, and only when he realized she was making her unsteady way to the door that would take her out of the east wing, did he find his voice again and say sharply, "Hold on a minute, Diana. Where do you think you're going?"

"Anywhere, as long as it's away from you," she said hoarsely.

"Not quite yet," he ruled, closing his fingers around the soft skin of her upper arm. "Not until you explain what you're doing here in the first place."

"I came looking for the truth, and I found it."

"And what truth is that?"

"You're a smart man," she replied with unvarnished scorn. "Figure it out for yourself."

A different kind of anger gripped him then, one directed entirely at himself. *This,* he raged silently, *is what happens when a man breaks his own rules, ignores the instincts that have guided him all his adult life and lets his hormones rule his mind. He loses perspective, along with his self-respect and damn near everything else he ever valued! You bloody fool, you've got exactly what you deserve!*

"I figured you out a long time ago, Diana," he replied bitterly. "I admit, you've got more class than most, but I got it right the first time when I realized that, at bottom, you're nothing but an underhanded opportunist."

Yanking her arm free, she rounded on him, spitting fire and fury. "Well, that makes two of us, then, doesn't it, because what kind of man keeps a shrine to his poor, barren dead wife, at the same time that he actively pursues a replacement who can give him what *she* could not?"

"What the hell are you talking about?"

"The fact that I'm nothing to you but a…a *womb!*"

So that was it! She'd snooped around and found out about Marie-Louise's inability to bear a child; the deep, dark motive the police had tried to pin on him, when they'd put him under suspicion for her death! "If a womb was all I wanted, I could take my pick from any number of women willing to lend me theirs—without my having to offer to marry them first," he informed her coldly. "You're sadly behind the times, Diana. Not only are the days of noblesse oblige long past, but there are recognized medical facilities offering everything a man needs to produce an heir, from in vitro fertilization of donor eggs to genetic surrogacy. I didn't ask you to become my wife because you happen to be pregnant with my child, although I'll admit that lent a certain urgency to my proposal. I asked because, foolishly, I thought we'd found something special and could make a good life together."

"Sure you did!" she shot back scathingly. "That's why, except for the night we had sex, you've never tried to be alone with me again, and why you never touch me or kiss me as if you mean it."

"You think I stayed away from you because I didn't want you?" He slapped the flat of his hand to his forehead. "For pity's sake, Diana, I'm a man, not a eunuch, and you're a beautiful, desirable woman. Even though you're woefully lacking in moral scruples, I've kept my distance because I want you so badly, I don't trust myself to be near you."

"You could have fooled me!"

"Apparently I fooled myself more. I refused to listen to my head, and followed my heart instead, even though I've suspected from day one that you've been lying to me and everyone else in this house. You didn't come here to recover from a broken marriage. You came to poke around in people's lives and dig up painful history, without any thought for the damage you might cause."

Her eyes bright with sudden tears, she cried, "Of course I thought about it! I never wanted to hurt anybody. I just wanted to get to the truth."

"Don't make me laugh," he said, disgust thick in his throat. "Sensationalism is the only truth people like you understand. But you picked on the wrong victim, this time. I had my fill of third-rate reporters when my wife died, and I'll be damned if I'll put up with one again."

She looked at him as if she thought he'd lost his mind. "What in the world are you raving about?"

"Tabloid journalism, what else? *Mon dieu,* you have the nerve to accuse me of not being able to let go of my dead wife, but it's you and your kind who won't let her rest in peace."

"You think that's why I'm here—to try to dig up dirt on your poor wife's death?"

He had to applaud her. Her voice fell to a shocked whisper of disbelief, and she gave an excellent imitation of a woman who'd had the wind knocked out of her. But hadn't he recognized from the first that she was very good at projecting just the right reaction to whatever situation she happened to find herself in? Suitably modest, when necessary? Swamped in misery, if the occasion called for it? Sweet as sugar, when it suited her to be?

"That's exactly why you're here, so spare me the wide-eyed innocent act, because it's not working any longer," he said harshly. "I might have lost my head long enough to sleep with you, but the damage to my brain was only temporary. It's functioning on all cylinders now."

She leaped at him then, and only his quick reflexes fended her off before her fingernails raked down his face. "You arrogant, ego-maniacal...*jerk!*" she wailed. "This isn't about you or your tragic past. It's about me, and my future."

"Meaning what, exactly? That you're willing to forfeit your career, if it means snagging me for a husband?"

She lifted her gaze to his, and the way she looked at him, as if seeing him clearly for the first time, filled him with self-loathing. Finally, in a small, defeated voice, she said, "I didn't come here to trap you in marriage, or harm you or your family in any way, Anton. I came looking for my birth mother. And I think I've found her."

"Here?" He wished he could reject her claim as the last-ditch attempt of a woman forced to resort to the outlandish in order to justify her actions, but the fight had gone out of her. Tears again filled her big blue eyes and rolled down her face. And he knew with sudden, blinding certainty, that she spoke the truth. "*Here,* Diana?" he repeated, more gently this time.

She nodded. "Don't ask me to name her," she sobbed. "I don't have the proof, or the right."

A flood of guilt washed over him at that. He, who prided himself on being a man of reason, had rushed home full of magnanimous forgiveness for sins she'd never committed. Yet, like the *imbecil* he undoubtedly was, it had taken him no time at all to leap to erroneous conclusions and condemn her accordingly.

Overcome with remorse, he caught her in his arms and drew her to his chest. Her heart fluttered against his, desperate as a bird trapped in a net. "Ah, Diana," he murmured, "don't you know you can tell me anything?"

"No," she sobbed. "You won't believe me. You don't trust me. You think I'm—"

He hushed her with his mouth, bringing it down on hers in

a desperate attempt to absorb her pain and absolve his guilt and let her know how sorry he was. She tasted of tears and despair, and all he intended was to let her know he was sorry for having misjudged her, not just tonight but from the very start.

What made him think he was above the weakness of other men, and that, once unleashed, the hunger he'd fought so hard to control would be satisfied with just a simple touch, a fleeting taste?

Heat roared through his blood, savage and unstoppable, reducing penitence to ashes. Driven past all sense of decency, he kissed her more deeply, persuaded his tongue between her lips and thrust it repeatedly into the sweet, dark recesses of her mouth.

She gave a little murmur. Her hands crept up around his neck. She leaned into him, aligning her soft curves to accommodate his hard angles. Flattening her breasts against the wall of his chest. Tilting her hips to cradle his erection against her belly.

It was too much, and not nearly enough. Almost immediately, he was throbbing, pulsing, embarrassingly close to ejaculating.

He lifted his mouth from hers. "Diana...?" he groaned urgently.

She opened her eyes, saw the agony in his, and knew what he was asking. "Yes," she breathed, on a soft sigh of surrender. "Yes. But please, Anton, not here."

"Of course not here," he said, and hoisting her in his arms, he carried her away from that haunted place to the sanctuary of his suite in the west wing.

CHAPTER TWELVE

HE KICKED his door closed, and with the blood thundering through his veins, took her, there in the foyer. Propping her up against the wall, he raised her nightgown with one hand, opened his fly with the other, and pushed himself between her thighs.

She parted them willingly, so wet and eager to receive him that, before he was fully inside her, the plump folds of her flesh were already rippling around him in anticipation of her climax. Helpless to stop them, she gasped aloud, buried her face at his throat and clutched the lapels of his jacket to keep herself upright.

This was madness. A man his age knew better than to be fumbling in a dark corner like a randy teenager at the mercy of his hormones. The bedroom lay no more than seven meters away, the study closer yet. But his body...hers...they weren't concerned with decorum or finesse. They cared only about banishing the ghosts that had come so close to dividing them.

He couldn't get enough of her. Wanted to lose himself completely in her tight, hot core. Sliding both hands under her buttocks, he lifted her up, the better to fill her. As instinctively as if she'd done it a thousand times before with him, and knew exactly his shape and texture and just what was needed to drive him wild, she locked her ankles in the small of his back, and widened her thighs further.

He sank deeper and again, he almost came. To prolong the

exquisite agony, he withdrew until just his tip rested inside her. At that, she wrapped her arms tightly around his neck. "Don't leave me, Anton," she begged.

He drove into her again. And again. Rocking wildly. Deeper, faster, his chest heaving, his heart hammering. "Never, *mon ange*," he promised hoarsely, teetering on the edge of sanity. "Not for as long as I have breath in my body."

Then his words were swallowed up by a mighty groan as the control he'd fought so hard to retain broke free in a shattering burst of passion, filling her with everything he had to give: his semen, his heart, his life.

He felt her shudder as the climax rolled over her. Held her tight as the spasms wrenched her body unmercifully. Whispered words of love in her ear as she screamed his name softly, over and over again, on a long-drawn out sigh, until at last she sank against him, spent and shivering.

Concerned, he said, "You're chilled, *mon amoureuse*."

"No," she insisted drowsily. "I'm warm right through to my soul."

But the goose bumps pebbling her skin said otherwise, and sliding out of her, he carried her to his bathroom, flicking on lamps as he passed. He filled the tub, helped her in, then stripping off his clothes, climbed in behind her and drew her back to lean against his chest.

"Do you feel up to talking, Diana?" he asked, smoothing his hands down her arms.

"Yes," she said, her voice soft as the murmur of a dove. "Talking is something that's long overdue between us."

"Will you tell me, then, why you went into the east wing?"

"To find out if what Sophie had told me was true."

"Ah, Sophie!" He expelled an irate sigh. "I should have guessed she had something to do with it. What did she say?"

"To begin with, she found out I'm pregnant by listening in on a private phone conversation I had with my best friend in the States. Afterward, she confronted me and said your wife had killed herself by jumping off the balcony outside your room, and that, at first, the police suspected you'd actually pushed her over the edge, because she couldn't give you children."

The malicious, interfering bitch! He'd have her out of his house at daybreak, if not sooner! "Was that all she said?"

"No…."

He heard the little catch in her breath that spoke of hesitation. "Tell me the rest, sweetheart," he urged. "Trust me to understand."

"She said that the only reason you were marrying me was that I was pregnant, and that once I'd given you an heir, you'd have no further use for me." Her voice dropped lower. "And that you'd never let me be part of our baby's life because I'm not upper-class enough." She turned so that her profile faced him. "I had to find out how much of what she told me was the truth."

"Yes, you did," he said. "But what a pity you didn't just come to me and ask."

"I didn't dare. The one time I questioned you about why you kept the east wing locked, you shut down on me completely."

"With good reason—or at least, it seemed so, at the time. When Marie-Louise died, the story made the front page of every tabloid in Europe. My ancient family name, which had never been tainted by scandal, was suddenly linked to a murder investigation, and the hyenas of every newspaper rag in Europe showed up in droves to feast on the carcass."

She linked her fingers with his and uttered a soft purr of sympathy. "Coping with that, on top of your wife's death, must have been unbearable."

"It was harder on my employees. At least I could lock the gates and keep the Press out. But they were waylaid as they left their homes, followed to work and hounded with questions. Anything they said was dissected for whatever scrap of juicy gossip it might contain, and you've been here long enough to know by now that the people of this village aren't used to dealing with journalists and don't realise how their words could be twisted and taken out of context. Gregoire, who is as loyal to me and my family as if he were my brother, felt the sting of that, more than most."

"Why? What did he do?"

"He made a statement to the effect that the news crews might as well pack up and move on to their next target, because there wasn't a man, woman or child in this area who would betray me or any member of my household, and whatever secrets might lie behind these walls would remain hidden forever."

"Oh dear! A well-intentioned, but misguided response, I'm sure, since everything there was to know had already made headlines."

"That's just the point. The biggest secret of all never did come out, but only because the entire village closed ranks around me until the scandal-seekers finally grew tired of being stone-walled and went away. But you have a right to hear it, and after you do, you might decide I'm not the man you want to marry, after all."

He saw how the stillness crept over her, how she tensed as if preparing herself for a blow, and wished it weren't so. But secrets had a way of coming out, no matter how deeply buried they might be, and if he hadn't known it before, he knew now that the past was never over until it was fully put to rest.

"The thing is, Diana, despite what Sophie led you to believe, Marie-Louise was driven by her own demons, not mine. Emotionally fragile, insecure and possessive, she saw a baby as a means to keep me by her side, even though she hated intimacy and shrank from my touch except for those times when she might conceive. Even then, the most she did was tolerate me."

Diana reached over her shoulder for his hand, and when he covered it with his, pressed a kiss to his fingers. "You don't have to go on, Anton," she said, her voice low. "I can hear how much it pains you to talk about this."

"I want you to know everything, *mon amoureuse,* and I want you to hear it from me."

She inclined her head in consent. "All right."

"I felt like one of my Arabian stallions, expected to perform when the time was right. For a man, that's not easy. We can't pretend, the way a woman can. Either we're aroused, and it shows, or we're not—and that shows, too. What began as love on my part, eventually turned to pity. For her, if she ever loved me at all, it turned to hatred. Her rages became more frequent and could be heard all over this house. The maids, especially the young ones, were afraid of her, and left to work elsewhere. I suggested we seek medical help and marriage counseling, both of which she refused. To put it bluntly, Diana, things got to the point where I'd had enough and told her I wanted a divorce. And the next morning, she…" He bowed his head and fought to keep the tremor out of his voice. "She threw herself off the parapet. I had gone riding in the hills on the other side of the village. When I returned, I found one of my gardeners covering her body with his shirt."

Diana maneuvered herself around until she was kneeling before him. "Oh, my poor Anton, I'm so very, very sorry! For both of you," she murmured, stroking his face tenderly, even as tears poured down her own.

He caught her hands and brought them to his mouth. When he could look at her again, he said, "I couldn't bear to go near the east wing, after that. The memories were too painful. If it had been possible, I'd have had it burned to the ground. Instead I locked it up and pretended it didn't exist."

"Until I came along and forced you to confront it again." She leaned her forehead against his. "Forgive me, Anton. I was wrong to go against your wishes."

"You were right," he said, drawing her to her feet. "You've made me face the past, and I can let it go now—the unhappiness, the guilt, the tragedy, the terrible, terrible waste of life and time. You've made me whole again, my lovely Diana."

She smiled shakily, and with a pang he saw how pale she was, how weary she looked. Lifting her out of the tub, he took a bath sheet from the heated towel rack and dried her still-slender, supple body. "I've kept you up too long," he said contritely. "It's past your bedtime."

She wilted against the vanity. "I am rather tired."

Quickly toweling himself off, he took her hand and led her to the big wide bed in his room. "Will you sleep with me tonight, my love?"

"Yes," she said simply. "Please."

He lifted her onto the mattress, lay down beside her, pulled the covers over the two of them and took her in his arms again. She curled up against him, warm, soft and content. "Keeping your poor wife's secret was such a decent thing to do," she said, on a stifled yawn. "A lot of men would have capitalized on it to earn public sympathy and clear themselves of criminal investigation."

"I had to keep quiet. If the story of her mental instability had ever leaked out, it would have killed her parents. She was their only child, and everything in the world to them."

She smothered another yawn. "Did they blame you for her death?"

"Yes, at first. What parents wouldn't? They wanted so badly to see her happy and thought I was the person who could make that happen. In the end, when her death was ruled accidental, they softened toward me, and it was kinder to leave them in ignorance of what really happened. They'd suffered enough. And more than enough had been said—as Gregoire learned to his cost. He discovered the hard way the wisdom of keeping his mouth shut."

Another yawn, more long drawn-out than the others, preceded her next question. "Is that why he's treated me with such cool reserve?"

"Quite possibly. Ever since that time, he's been uneasy around strangers who show up for no apparent reason. In fact, he was so shaken by the fall-out from his off-the-cuff remarks after the tragedy that he tendered his resignation and offered to leave the area completely. Of course, I refused to accept it."

"Oh, I'm so glad you did," she murmured drowsily. "Otherwise, I might never have found my mother."

The next moment, she was asleep. Her lashes rested thick and dark against her cheeks, her breathing grew deep and regular, and the hand she'd stroked up and down his chest lay limp against his skin.

But for him, what she'd let slip, in those last moments before she drifted off, hit Anton with the impact of a thunderbolt booming through the quiet night.

So that's it! he thought, all the disparate pieces of her story suddenly coming together in his mind and making perfect sense. *How the devil did I miss seeing it before?*

She awoke to sunshine, a rosemary and lavender scented breeze fluttering through the open windows, and the uncanny sense that she was being watched. Opening her eyes, she found Anton stretched out on his side next to her, with his head propped up on his hand. "Good morning," he said. "Remember me?"

"Mmm-hmm." She blinked groggily, and wondered why she was naked, but he was freshly shaved and fully dressed in tailored gray trousers and a cream shirt. "What time is it?"

"Almost ten."

"Ten?" Clutching the sheet to her breasts, she went to sit up, then wished she hadn't as nausea swept over her. Swallowing, she said, "But it's Wednesday. The first tour group will be here in an hour. I need to get moving."

"Uh-uh. I fired you, remember, and we have other business to take care of today." He eased her back against the pillows. "Right now, though, you're looking a little green, *ma belle*. Will the tea and dry toast I ordered help settle your stomach?"

"I hope so," she groaned, then, as the import of his remark

struck home, started up from the pillows again. "You ordered tea and toast to be brought *here,* to your room? For me? Good grief, Anton, you'll have your entire household buzzing!"

He swung off the bed and went to the breakfast tray waiting on his dresser. "Jeanne is the only one I spoke to, and I can rely on her discretion," he said, pouring tea into a cup and bringing it to her. "And what does it matter, anyway? Everyone's going to know you're pregnant before much longer, and as far as I'm concerned, the sooner the better. I'm done with secrets."

"Me, too," she said evasively, knowing she still harbored a big one of her own. But how best to share it—and with whom? Jeanne, or Anton?

He dropped a kiss on her nose. "Good," he said, and glanced at his watch. "How long will it take, do you think, before you feel well enough to get dressed and meet me in my office?"

"Half an hour, or so. Why?"

"I want to take care of that business I just mentioned," he said easily, a mysterious half smile touching his mouth. "Shall we say eleven o'clock?"

She searched his face, looking for a hint of what he meant, but he was giving nothing away. Probably he'd arranged for her to meet his lawyer, maybe to sign a prenuptial agreement or the like. It was a common enough occurrence these days. He was, after all, a very wealthy man, and although she was hardly a pauper, her assets didn't begin to compare to his.

"Okay," she said equably. "I'll be there."

CHAPTER THIRTEEN

WEARING nothing but a badly wrinkled nightgown, and scooting down the hall to her own suite undetected, took some doing, but Diana managed it without being seen. By eleven, she'd showered, shampooed and dried her hair, and showed up outside Anton's office shortly after, wearing a cool blue cotton dress loose-fitting enough to disguise her ever-so-slightly thickened waistline.

He opened the door immediately when she knocked and ushered her inside. To her utter shock, she found Jeanne and Gregoire seated in club chairs around a low table at the far end of the room, and a ripple of apprehension skimmed over her.

Swinging her gaze to Anton, she said, "What's this all about? What's going on here, Anton?"

He put his arm around her shoulders. "Forgive me, my love, but I'm afraid you've been set up."

"So it would appear," she said. "The question is, why?"

He shrugged. "I could think of no other way to introduce you to your biological parents."

Parents? Not mother, but *parents?*

The room swam dizzily. The floor rose up to meet her. Staggering, she groped blindly for the nearest solid object, and would have fallen had he not caught her securely and steered her safely to one of the remaining club chairs.

"That was clumsy of me," he whispered, pushing her head down between her knees. "Forgive me again, *ma trés chère Dianne.*"

She drew in deep, reviving breaths, dimly aware that Jeanne and Gregoire had sprung up from their seats. Opening her eyes, she saw their feet close to hers and felt another hand against her back, small and feminine. "Bring her a glass of water, Gregoire," she heard her mother say.

At length, the room stopped spinning and she was able to lift her head. Gregoire knelt before her, his eyes filled with concern. Blue eyes, just like hers. No wonder she hadn't recognized them sooner. She'd been looking at the wrong face.

"Here, *ma fille,*" he said, offering the glass.

She had to hold it in both hands because she was shaking so badly, but the ice cold water helped restore her. "I don't understand," she said, when she could speak.

Anton dropped into the chair next to hers, while Jeanne and Gregoire resumed theirs. "That's why I asked you to come here. So that we could explain."

She slewed a resentful glare his way. "You mean to say, you knew all along, and you didn't say a word to me?"

"I knew only part of the story, and it wasn't mine to tell," he said. "Where you fit into it was something I learned only last night."

"Last night?" She frowned. He'd been with her, last night. "How?"

"Because you told me."

"I did no such thing!"

He made a pitiful effort not to smile, and failed miserably. "You don't remember, do you?"

"No, I can't say I do."

"We were talking about the publicity after Marie-Louise died, and I mentioned that Gregoire had wanted to resign his position here and move away, but I'd talked him out of it. The last thing you said before you fell asleep was you were glad he didn't because—"

"Because, if he had, I'd never have found my mother." The memory came back hazily, but too real to be a dream. "I remember it now."

She looked at Jeanne and Gregoire. They were holding hands, and Jeanne was crying. Swinging her attention back to Anton, she said, "But I still don't understand why you say you already knew part of the story."

He threw a questioning glance at Gregoire. "It's up to you to tell her, my friend."

Briefly Gregoire lowered his eyes. When he looked up again, they were dull with pain. "I am fifty-one," he began. "Six years older than Jeanne. But she was only sixteen when we fell in love, and so although we promised ourselves to one another, we kept our affair secret because, in those days, a man my age would have been horse-whipped for seducing so young a girl.

"Then, one day, I received a letter from her, telling me it was over between us, and she'd left Bellevue-sur-Lac for a better life somewhere more exciting. Angry, heartbroken, at a loss to know what to do next, I buried myself in my work and learned as much as I could about viniculture, but deep in my bones I never accepted that a love such as ours had died for no apparent reason."

"But there *was* a reason," Jeanne said, taking over the story. "I had discovered I was pregnant. My Gregoire was admired, well respected, building a successful career for himself and he would have lost everything if it had become known that he was my lover—perhaps even his life, because my brothers were fiercely protective of me. I loved him too much to let that happen, and so…"

She stopped and began to cry again, helplessly, bitterly. "And so," she sobbed, when she was able to continue, "I didn't tell him I was pregnant. Instead I ran away to Aix, to a convent for unmarried mothers, and although it broke my heart, when my baby was born, I gave her up for adoption, and then I came home again."

"What happened next?" Diana asked, not even realizing she was crying, too, until Anton plucked a tissue from a box on the table, mopped at her tears and draped a comforting arm around her shoulders. "Did you tell him what you'd done?"

"Not for a long time. I was afraid, and so I avoided him whenever I could. Of course, we ran into one another often. It's impossible to hide from anyone in a village as small as ours. But one day, we met by accident down by the lake. It was my baby's first birthday, and I had gone there because I was so sad and didn't want to be with other people.

"He had been fishing, and saw me when he brought in his boat. There was no one else there, just the cold winter wind and the gray sky, and suddenly all those feelings we'd both repressed just rushed up to the surface. The next moment, we were in each other's arms, and I was telling him why I had left him, and begging him to forgive me."

She lifted her tear-stained gaze to Diana, haggard heartbreak shadowing her eyes. "And now, I must beg for yours, Diana. Because, as you have suspected for so long, you are the child I gave away, although I didn't know it until this morning when Anton came to us and told us what he'd learned."

"If you must blame someone," Gregoire put in, a terrible emptiness in his eyes also, "then blame me. I am the one who made your mother pregnant, and it was because of me that she placed you for adoption. What it has cost her in silent sorrow and private tears over the years, only I know. I can tell you that she has paid dearly. We both have."

"Not you, surely," Diana said doubtfully. "You don't even like me."

"I saw the interest you took in my wife, and at first, it's true, I didn't trust you," he admitted. "But then I became suspicious for a different reason. Sometimes, a certain look about you, the way you laughed, the expression on your face, even the way you walked, they struck a familiar note."

"I thought the same thing, when I first met you," Anton interrupted, "but I was looking elsewhere for the reason and didn't make the connection."

Gregoire nodded. "For myself, I began to wonder, could it be? Had a miracle occurred? It didn't seem possible. Our child was born in France, and you were American."

"My adoptive father was a professor of law and spent a year on an exchange program, teaching at the university in Aix," she told him. "He and my mother—my other mother," she amended, "adopted me shortly before they returned to America."

"That explains it, then." Her father shook his head, as though he couldn't believe how all the pieces of the puzzle suddenly made sense. "I waited for you to declare yourself, but you never did, and my Jeanne had suffered enough, wondering if every young woman your age might be her daughter. She denied herself more children because of what she had done to you. I couldn't raise her hopes by sharing my suspicions with her, only to have them proved groundless. So I said nothing— not because I didn't like you, Diana, but because I was afraid I'd grow to like you too much."

"I don't know what to say." She stared at them all, helplessly. "Two months ago, I was alone in the world. Now I've found not only my biological mother, but my father, too. I have a fiancé, and I'm expecting a baby in—oh!" She stopped and flung a nervous glance at Anton.

"They know," he said, clasping her hand. "I've confessed, and your father's promised not to shoot me. And, sweetheart, we all understand it's a lot for you to take in."

"But I still don't understand where you fit into it, Anton."

"I've known Jeanne and Gregoire's side of the story ever since I took over the running of the estate, and my aunts have known it even longer."

"We couldn't allow the de Valoises to place such trust in us, without their knowing what we'd done," her father said. "Even the best-kept secrets sometimes have a way of coming out and hurting people. We respect this family too much to risk having such a thing happen to them."

"You see?" Anton stroked the back of his hand up her cheek. "Your parents are smarter than we are, Diana. They realized a long time ago something we've only just learned. You have to trust the people you care about."

She glanced from him to her parents. They sat tensely, their hands clinging together, their faces full of hope and full of fear, and she wondered why she was holding back, when all she wanted was to let them know how glad she was to have found them.

"I've been looking for you for so long," she said, her voice quavering helplessly, "and by some miracle, I've found you. As far as I'm concerned, from this day on, you're my mom and dad."

She felt it then, the unconditional love she'd always longed for. It showered over her, in the feel of the arms around her, in the tears they shed and the words they murmured.

They celebrated that night, with a formal, eight-course dinner and champagne for everyone, including the nonalcoholic kind for her. Even Sophie was invited because, when he heard she'd made arrangements to fly to Lisbon the next day, Anton relented and allowed her to stay at the château one more night.

Diana took pains to look her best, pinning up her hair and putting on the one evening gown she'd brought with her, a strapless number of softly draped silk chiffon that might have been designed for a woman in early pregnancy.

"Radiantly beautiful and needing only one more thing to make you perfect," Anton murmured huskily, when he stopped by her room to accompany her downstairs. Then, turning her around, he slipped something cool and smooth around her neck, and urged her toward the mirror. "These belonged to my mother, and I know she'd want you to wear them tonight. What do you think?"

"That you're going to make me cry again," she said, stunned by the beauty of the delicate layered diamond necklace glinting against her skin in the lamplight.

"Then prepare to cry often, because this is just the first of more good things to come."

"You don't have to buy me expensive baubles," she whispered, loving him with her eyes. If ever a man was made to wear black tie, it was her handsome fiancé. "I have you, and that's enough to make me happy."

Everyone else had gathered in the drawing room when they arrived, including her parents. Despite their reservations, Anton insisted they join the party.

"But I'm your housekeeper!" her mother had objected.

"You're also my future mother-in-law, Jeanne," he'd reminded her. "And that means some things are going to change around here, so you'd better get used to the idea."

"Well, of course, Josette and I knew you were pregnant," Hortense confided gleefully, taking Diana aside as they all trooped into the dining room. "You have that luminous look about you. And my darling, we're delighted. I've never seen Anton happier."

Not surprisingly, when she heard of Diana's connection to her cousin's housekeeper and head vintner, Sophie had to get in one last malicious dig. "Poor Marie-Louise wasn't up to much," she muttered behind her hand, "but at least she came with the right pedigree."

"Sophie, why don't you do us all a favor and stick a fork in your eye?" Josette suggested sweetly, a remark that promptly reduced Hortense to quivering hysterics.

Well, one thing was certain, Diana decided, unable to keep her own face straight. Life would never be dull, as long the aunts were around to keep things entertaining.

* * *

Later, when the excitement had died down and the château had settled into silence, he'd drawn her along the upper hall to his suite and locked the door behind him. "Tomorrow," he promised, "you'll decide which rooms are to be ours after we're married, and how you want them furnished. But you're spending tonight here, with me."

All through dinner, he'd watched her, impatient to be alone with her, yet enjoying seeing her glow in the affection of her parents and his aunts. Now, as she lay naked on his bed, with him sitting beside her, naked also, he watched her again, hungry and desperate to make love to her. But he was determined that, tonight, he would do so at leisure, with none of the frantic haste that had marked their previous encounters.

Flushing, she said, "You're staring," and went to turn off the bedside lamp.

"Don't," he said, forcing the word past the thickness in his throat. "Let me look at you. I want to see you when you come, when I touch you here…and here."

With slow reverence he skimmed her shoulders, her breasts, her hips, her thighs. Her skin was warm, and smooth as cream. And with every brush of his hand, encroaching passion flooded her until she was stained the color of rosé wine, and begging him with inarticulate little cries to fill her with his powerful strength.

"Easy, *mon trésor,* the night is long and all ours," he murmured, eluding her when she reached out to cradle his throbbing flesh, and dipped his head to press a kiss to the side of her mouth, to take the tip of one rosy nipple between his teeth and nip gently. "I have something to give you, first. I saw these in a shop in Toulouse, and knew they were meant for you."

Without taking his eyes from her face, he reached into the bedside table drawer and withdrew a black velvet sack. Loosening its drawstring with his teeth, he pulled out the long rope of pearls and let it fall softly at her throat. It rolled over her breasts, coiled sweetly in the hollow of her navel, slipped lower to her belly, then slithered to the mattress and nested against the side of her thigh. And everywhere it went, his tongue followed, dancing lightly over her skin until she was thrashing her head back and forth with need and clawing at his shoulders.

"What is it you want me to do?" he asked, adoring her with his eyes. "Tell me how to please you, Diana."

She groped wildly for his hand, and drew it between her legs. "Touch me here," she begged. "Please, Anton, I need to feel you here."

"Oui," he said, and with a single deft caress of his finger, brought her to the brink of orgasm. Then he lowered his head and stroked her with his tongue, and she arched off the bed with a strangled cry.

"Oui," he said again, lifting his head. "Just so, *mon cherie.*" And he brought to the brink a third time, feathering his tongue over the sensitized nub of flesh at her center until she splintered like crystal into a thousand prisms of sparkling ecstasy. Then, with the aftershocks still rippling over her, he buried himself in her sleek folds, and loved her with everything he had to give.

When it was over, and she lay panting and glistening beside him, he cradled her to his heart, and the words he'd been too proud to say before came easily to him because, after all was said and done, they were the only truth that counted. "I love you, Diana," he whispered.

She looked up at him, the rise and fall of her breasts, the sultry droop of her eyelashes, a promise in themselves that, this time, he had chosen well. Theirs would be a marriage made in heaven, and in bed, as well.

"I'm so glad," she replied softly. "Because I love you, too. With all my heart."

EPILOGUE

2:00 p.m., March 21

THEY came to the hospital in Aix to visit her and the baby, a steady stream of people, and every one related in one way or another. Aunts, uncles, cousins, they brought flowers and candy and fruit, and little hand-made gifts for her son.

They shook Anton by the hand, and hugged her. "We're so glad you found your way home," they whispered. "Look at your mother and father! You've made them smile again."

Stirring in his bassinet, the baby let out a squeak. "Stay put!" Hortense cried, pressing Diana back against the pillows when she reached for him. "I'll hand him over. You had a rough time of it, last night, and need to take it easy."

Seated on her other side, Anton leaned close. Touched her hair, her face, his gaze hungry. "I want to be alone with you and our son."

"Me, too," she murmured, "but we have the rest of our lives together."

"Even so, tell me if this rush of visitors gets to be too much, and I'll send everyone packing. You've been through enough in the last twenty-four hours…" He cleared his throat. Blinked his gorgeous gray eyes rapidly. "*I've* put you through enough."

She smiled and cupped his jaw. This proud, indomitable

husband of hers, who'd never backed down from a challenge in his life, had had a hard time of it, seeing her in the throes of childbirth. "*Mon dieu*, how much more can she stand?" he'd asked wretchedly, when at last she reached the final stages of delivery and was struggling to push their baby out into the world.

"Courage, *mon ami*," the doctor had urged. "Your wife is magnificent!"

She hadn't felt magnificent, not then, with the sweat dripping from her hair and rolling down her face. Giving birth wasn't glamorous, but oh, it was beautiful and exhilarating! And now, bathed and perfumed, with the green hospital gown exchanged for a fine cotton nightgown embroidered in silk, her eight-and-a-half-pound baby safe in her arms, and her husband gazing at her as if she were the most extraordinary woman ever to walk the earth, she felt like a goddess.

"We made this baby together, my darling man," she reminded him, "and he's worth every minute of hard labor it took to bring him here."

At that moment, a nurse appeared at the door of her private room, which was just as well. The look on Anton's face, the hunger in his gaze as it slid over Diana...well, it had been a week or more since they'd last made love, and the strain was beginning to tell!

"Too many visitors in here," the nurse declared, shooing away everyone but Anton, his aunts and her parents, before ushering in Henri. "Immediate family only from now on, please, although I will allow this man a few minutes. He's been waiting patiently for the last half hour for his turn to indulge in a little baby worship."

"I was wondering where you were," Diana said, holding out her hand in welcome. "Come here and say hello to your great-nephew. He looks a little like you, don't you think?"

"Not from everything I've heard," her uncle said, dropping a slow wink Anton's way. "This one's a de Valois to the core—

with a bit of his mother's beauty thrown in for good measure, so I'm told."

She laughed. "Oh, very diplomatic, *mon oncle,* but then, you always did know just the right thing to say! What's in that basket you're carrying?"

"Bouillabaisse and bread still warm from the oven. Better than that abominable stuff they try to pass off as food in this place. I've brought enough for all of you, and your Tante Solange baked lemon tarts for dessert." He looked over his shoulder furtively. "I even smuggled in a bottle of champagne to celebrate the little one's safe arrival."

Very much the protective new grandfather, Gregoire said, "I'm not sure that's such a good idea. Diana's nursing, and champagne might not agree with the baby."

"What do you know about babies?" Henri scoffed good-naturedly. "*I* am the expert here, and I tell you, *mon ami,* a Frenchman is never too young to appreciate good champagne, and we now know that this young fellow is French through and through."

Diana shared a smiling glance with Anton.

I love you, he mouthed silently.

I love you, too, she telegraphed back, filled with a wonderful sense of peace and contentment. "It's okay, Dad," she said. "I don't need champagne to celebrate. I have my family. It's all I ever wanted, and more than enough for me."

If you enjoyed what you just read,
then we've got an offer you can't resist!

Take 2 bestselling love stories FREE!

Plus get a FREE surprise gift!

Clip this page and mail it to Harlequin Reader Service®

IN U.S.A.	IN CANADA
3010 Walden Ave.	P.O. Box 609
P.O. Box 1867	Fort Erie, Ontario
Buffalo, N.Y. 14240-1867	L2A 5X3

YES! Please send me 2 free Harlequin Presents® novels and my free surprise gift. After receiving them, if I don't wish to receive anymore, I can return the shipping statement marked cancel. If I don't cancel, I will receive 6 brand-new novels every month, before they're available in stores! In the U.S.A., bill me at the bargain price of $3.80 plus 25¢ shipping & handling per book and applicable sales tax, if any*. In Canada, bill me at the bargain price of $4.47 plus 25¢ shipping & handling per book and applicable taxes**. That's the complete price and a savings of at least 10% off the cover prices—what a great deal! I understand that accepting the 2 free books and gift places me under no obligation ever to buy any books. I can always return a shipment and cancel at any time. Even if I never buy another book from Harlequin, the 2 free books and gift are mine to keep forever.

106 HDN DZ7Y
306 HDN DZ7Z

Name	(PLEASE PRINT)	
Address	Apt.#	
City	State/Prov.	Zip/Postal Code

Not valid to current Harlequin Presents® subscribers.

Want to try two free books from another series?
Call 1-800-873-8635 or visit www.morefreebooks.com.

* Terms and prices subject to change without notice. Sales tax applicable in N.Y.
** Canadian residents will be charged applicable provincial taxes and GST.
All orders subject to approval. Offer limited to one per household.
® are registered trademarks owned and used by the trademark owner and or its licensee.

PRES04R   ©2004 Harlequin Enterprises Limited

HARLEQUIN Presents

UNcut

Even more passion for your reading pleasure!

Escape into a world of intense passion and scorching
romance! Everything you've always loved in
Harlequin Presents books, but we've turned up
the thermostat just a little, so that the relationships
really sizzle....

Kimberley's little boy is in danger, and the only person
who can help is his father. But Luc doesn't even know
his son exists. The gorgeous Brazilian tycoon will help—
provided Kimberley sleeps with him....

MILLION-DOLLAR
LOVE-CHILD

by Sarah Morgan

Available November 2006.
Don't miss it!

HARLEQUIN *Presents*